Blacks
in the Annals of
Church
History

Blacks
in the Annals of
Church
History

Emmanuel Kofi Bonney, CA (Ghana), AAIA (UK), M.Min., M.Sc., B.A.

Kravitz & Sons
INNOVATORS IN PUBLISHING, MARKETING AND ADVERTISING

Kravitz and Sons LLC
1301 Farmville Blvd, Suite 104
Greenville, NC 27834

Published by Kravitz and Sons LLC.

ISBN: 979-8-89639-318-4 (sc)
ISBN: 979-8-89639-317-7 (e)

Library of Congress Control Number: 2025911016

Because of the dynamic nature of the Internet, any web addresses or links contained in this book may have changed since publication and may no longer be valid. The views expressed in this work are solely those of the author and do not necessarily reflect the views of the publisher, and the publisher hereby disclaims any responsibility for them.

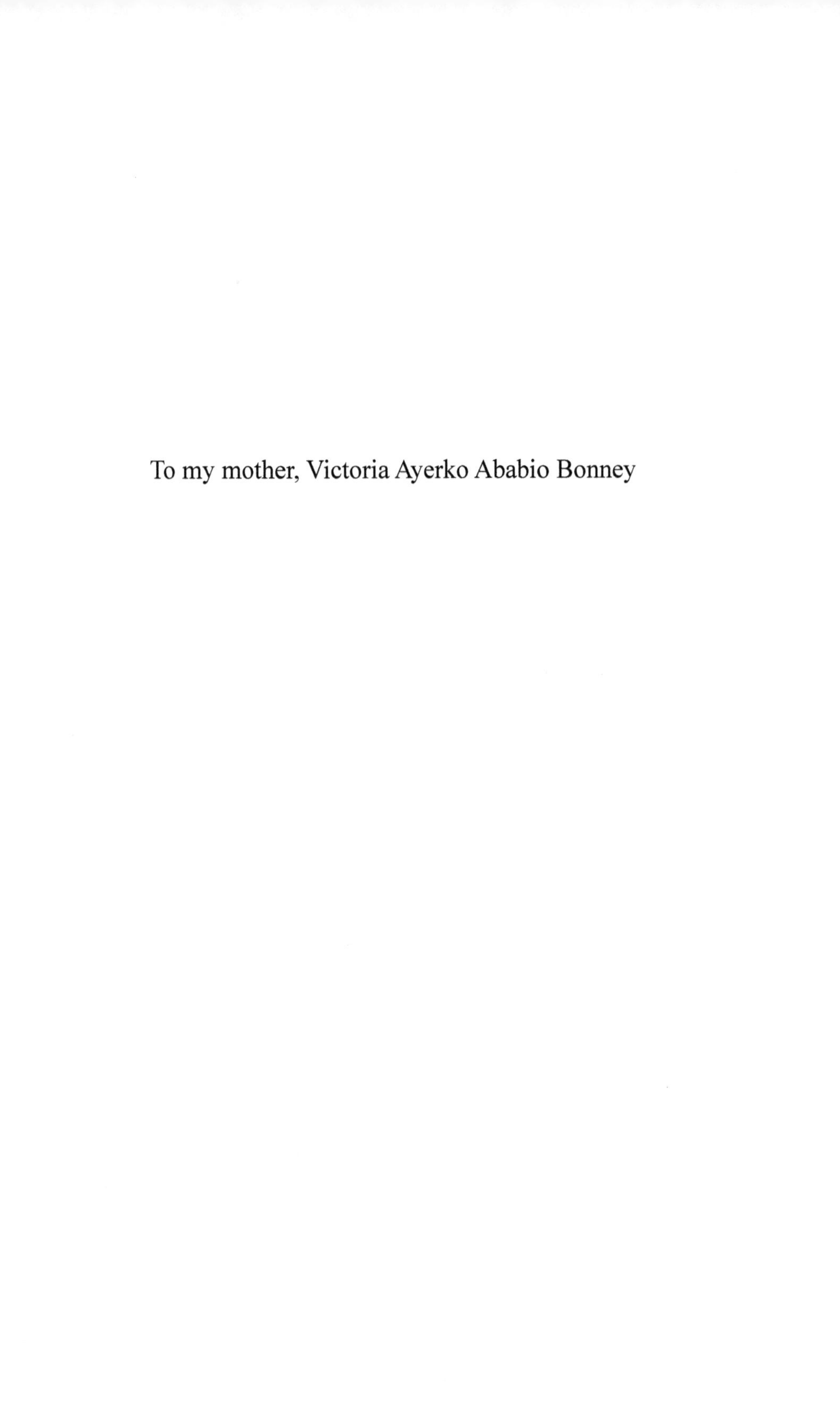

To my mother, Victoria Ayerko Ababio Bonney

"In the beginning, male and female He created them, black and white He formed them."

Contents

FOREWORD

Serendipitous surprises encounter us in life's pathway. One still stands out in my memory, that is, the continuing relationships through the years with many former students from the southeastern part of the nation. The connection began when Dr. Sam Chand, president of Beulah Heights University, graciously invited Southwestern Christian University Graduate School, where I served as dean, to conduct classes on the Atlanta campus. This began a beautiful relationship where students could complete their master of ministry degree from Southwestern, located in Oklahoma City, by taking their classes at Beulah Heights as well as at Southwestern. As a result, my life has been enriched by all the wonderful and outstanding students from many countries of the world.

Franklin Kofi Bonney, now Emmanuel Kofi Bonney, stood out in his class at that time. His character and persona, as well as his passion for truth, set him apart. His professional and academic achievements are many, but Emmanuel walks in great humility and strong Christian faith. Professors love lifelong learners, and Emmanuel was such a student as indicated in this recent book, *Blacks in the Annals of Church History*. His historical and biblical research cites the great contributions of many outstanding blacks in the world. You will meet them on the pages of this book. Also included are pictures, diagrams, and maps of ancient cities. His bibliography will direct readers to many unfamiliar sources.

Emmanuel's studies make a valuable perspective to the current racial, ethnic, and social debates. Although the Bible teaches, we are all one in Adam, those of us who are not black will learn much by reading and studying this book. I highly recommend it and pray we all come together as one.

Dr. Garnet E. Pike, Former Dean

Southwestern Christian University Graduate School, Oklahoma City, Oklahoma

PREFACE

Song of Songs or Song of Solomon 1:5–6 (New American Bible Revised Edition) (NABRE)[3] reads,

Love's Boast

I am black and beautiful,

Daughters of Jerusalem

Like the tents of Qedar,

like the curtains of Solomon.

Do not stare at me because I am so black

because the sun has burned me.

The sons of my mother were angry with me;

they charged me with the care of the vineyards:

my own vineyard I did not take care of.

The story of a black or dark-skinned person is fascinating and intriguing. Why is the person black or dark-skinned? How did that black person end up in the Bible, Song of Songs, or Song of Solomon, which forms part of the books of the Holy Scriptures? Do blacks have a history? How long have blacks been in existence? And what are blacks' contributions to church history, if any? In any case, when did the church begin?

The above questions and many others bugged my mind for a long time so I set myself to find answers to them, and the result of my research is this little book, which I hope has brought out some of the contributions of blacks to world history, especially blacks' contributions to church history.

Blacks in the Annals of Church History

ACKNOWLEDGMENTS

My immeasurable thanks go to Jehovah the Almighty God, Jesus Christ of Nazareth, my Lord and Savior, and the Holy Spirit for making it possible for me to write this book.

My thanks also go to Raphael E. Arku, ScD, for obtaining copyright permission for an image in the book and also for helping me put the sketches in PowerPoint.

A very special thanks to my dear wife, Edith, for helping me check the accuracy of quotations in the book as well as proofreading the manuscript and to my children—Richard, Rosemond, Comfort, and Divine—and my grandchildren for their encouragement when working on the manuscript.

I would also like to thank Dr. Garnet Pike, former dean of the Graduate School of Southwestern Christian University, Oklahoma City, for inculcating in us students the need to "finish well." His words always ring in my mind and heart, giving me impetus "to break the mold and bridge the gap."

Finally, my thanks go to Tom Taylor, Sunday school teacher at The Church of the Apostles, Atlanta, Georgia, for his encouragement in having this book published and to the entire production team of Kravitz & Sons, LLC who made the publication possible.

INTRODUCTION

The Beginning of the Church

The church began from the beginning of creation. Revelation 13:8 (NIV) reads, "All inhabitants of the earth will worship the beast—all whose names have not been written in the Lamb's book of life, the Lamb who was slain from the creation of the world."[5]

What does that verse imply? It is saying, among other things, that before male and female were created (Genesis 1:26–27),[1] before God formed Adam (Genesis 2:7) and Eve (Genesis 2:22), and before they became living souls and inhabited the earth with their offspring, Jesus Christ of Nazareth, the Lamb of God, had already been sacrificed for the redemption of mankind.

The Church at the Foundation of the World

God, being omnipotent, omniscient, and omnipresent, knew beforehand that Adam and Eve would sin and the sin would adversely affect their descendants and all of creation, so He made provision for their redemption before they were created and became living souls and eventually sinned. What was the sin? It was the sin of disobedience and stubbornness. "For rebellion *is as* the sin of witchcraft, And stubbornness *is as* iniquity and idolatry" (1 Samuel 15:23, italics in the original).[36] God gave Adam and, by extension, Eve a simple command not to eat the fruit of the tree that gave knowledge of good and evil or they would die in the day that they ate it (Genesis 2:15–17).

---

[1] All biblical citations, unless otherwise noted, are from the Holy Bible, New King James Version.

At the time God gave Adam the commandment, Eve had not yet been formed. Therefore, she was not physically present when the commandment was given. Since she knew the commandment and even quoted it in her own way to the serpent (Genesis 3:2–3), Adam might have told her. In any case, she was in Adam when God gave the commandment so she was as well bound by it (see Hebrews 7:1–10). They disobeyed God at the instigation of Satan, who disguised himself as a serpent, and did what they were told not to do and died. They died spiritually in their sins and trespasses (Ephesians 2:1) the same day they ate the fruit as God said they would because God's word does not return to Him void without achieving the purpose for which it is sent (Isaiah 55:10– 11).

Even though Adam "lived" for 930 years (Genesis 5:5), he was just like a zombie in the sight of God. Besides, God does not count days like men do. A thousand years are like a day, and a day is like a thousand years (2 Peter 3:8) in His sight. Interestingly, no human being has ever lived for a thousand years since creation. The person who lived the longest, Methuselah, died at the age of 969 years (Genesis 5:27). Through Adam and Eve's sin, God "lost" (Luke 19:10) His entire creation because everything He created was tainted by their sin, yet He has called-out ones.

The called-out ones are the sons and daughters of humans, irrespective of the color of their skin, and are called the church. The church is a spiritual entity and an assembly of human beings, those who do the commandments of God and have washed their robes in the blood of the Lamb and have the right to eat the fruit of the Tree of Life (Revelation 22:14).

Since the church comprises people of different skin colors, one may ask: What was Adam's skin color? And what was Eve's skin color? The answer to these questions is very simple: Adam's skin color was black, or dark, and Eve's skin color was white. How do we know? We know because the Scriptures say that God took the dust of the earth to form the man but took a bone from the man's ribs to form the woman. The man was formed out of raw material; the woman was formed from a bone from the man who had already been formed. Therefore, whereas Adam's skin color was just like the color of the dust of the earth from which he was formed, Eve's skin color was white though not white like calico (British) or chalk because she was formed from a finished product.

So in the beginning, male and female He created them, black and white He formed them. And their offspring were also black males and white females just as they were. The females were so fair that Genesis 6:1–2 (KJV) says,

> And it came to pass, when men began to multiply on the face of the earth, and daughters were born unto them, That the sons of God saw the daughters of men that they were fair; and they took them wives of all which they chose.[4]

Over time, however, due to their DNA mutation, they started producing black females and white males as well. So the black females and the black males and the white females and white males started pairing away, resulting in the concentration of all-blacks and all-whites in specific locations on the earth. Whites, blacks, and any color in between therefore have come from the first black, or dark-skinned, man, Adam.

Now, if the Redeemer, the Lamb of God, were slain from the foundation of the world but the universe was created before Adam and Eve were spiritually created and physically formed, then it stands to reason that the church began before Adam and Eve came into existence. If so, why did it come into existence before human beings were created?

Protoevangelium

When Adam and Eve sinned, God was not taken by surprise. He simply activated the provision He had already made for their redemption as recorded in Revelation 13: 8 verbalizing the first good news known as "Protoevangelium," or "Protevangelium," in Christian theology in Genesis 3:15 when speaking to the serpent, "And I will put enmity Between you and the woman, And between your seed and her Seed; He shall bruise your head, And you shall bruise His heel."

It is noteworthy that God put the enmity between the seed of the woman and the seed of the serpent not between the seed of the man and the seed of the serpent or between the seed of the woman and the man and the seed of the serpent. This enmity between the seed of the woman and the seed of the serpent is being played out since Cain killed his brother Abel when only two of the woman and the man's male offspring were in existence. Even though both children were born by the same woman after the man had known her, the sharp distinction between good and evil was on display immediately, the antitype of the enmity between the seed of the woman and the seed of the serpent.

Throughout the ages, there has been an ongoing battle between good and evil personified in human beings who represent the seed of the woman and the seed of the serpent. This battle, which is actually between the offspring of the woman and the offspring of the serpent (Satan), has been intensified after the birth of the offspring of the woman whom she conceived by the Holy Spirit. These two seeds are represented by the church and the synagogue of Satan, but Jesus, the seed of the woman, said, "I will build My church, and the gates of Hades [Hell] shall not prevail against it" (Matthew 16:18b). The children of darkness can never prevail against the children of light.

Since the church began from the foundation of the world and the seed of the woman (Jesus Christ of Nazareth) proclaimed that He had "come to seek and save that which was lost" (Luke 19:10 KJV), were blacks involved in the building of His church? If yes, how?

Answers to the above questions and many others are the focus of this book. It is hoped that the reader will enjoy the trip as we go along.

CHAPTER 1

THE FLOOD OF NOAH

As we have seen previously, God commanded Adam and Eve not to eat the fruit of the tree in the midst of the garden that gave knowledge of good and evil, but Adam and his wife, Eve, disobeyed God and ate the forbidden fruit. God then sentenced them to death for their disobedience (Genesis 3:19). Death is therefore not a gateway to heaven. It is a punishment for sin. "For the wages of sin *is* death, but the gift of God *is* eternal life in Christ Jesus our Lord" (Romans 6:23) (italics in the original).

This is true because when God created Adam and Eve, He did not tell them that one day they would die and come to Him anywhere. He rather gave them dominion over all creation, blessed them, and commanded them to multiply and fill the earth, spreading over the face of the entire earth (Genesis 1:27–28). It was God who visited Adam and Eve in the cool of the day, not the other way round (Genesis 3:8). Besides that, in Revelation 21:3, it is written that the tabernacle of God will be among the people and He will dwell with them (not the other way round) and be their God (see Revelation 21:1–3). Therefore, as it was in the beginning, so it will be at the end. A world without end! Sin is missing the mark.

After the death sentence was passed on Adam and Eve, Adam knew (had sexual intercourse with) his wife, and they had a son whom they named Cain, meaning "spear,"[32] in Hebrew. Later they had another son they named Abel, meaning "Breath," or "son" or "breathing spirit" in Hebrew.[30] Cain killed Abel out of jealousy because, at a worship of the Creator (God), his offering was not accepted, but Abel's was (Genesis 4:1–8). When he was nursing the thought of killing his brother, God warned him that sin was waiting at his door to consume him (Genesis 4:6–7) so he should refrain from his evil plan, but he paid no heed. He went ahead and murdered his brother in cold blood. That is the beginning of untold human atrocities in the world as a result of religious differences and jealousy. For Cain's punishment, God banished him from His presence. Therefore, the punishment for killing people on religious grounds is eternal banishment from the presence of God and being thrown into the lake which burns with fire and brimstone known as the second death (Revelation 20:12–15, 21: 8), if such sin and/or other iniquities are not forgiven through Jesus Christ of Nazareth before one's death.

Why was Abel's offering accepted but Cain's was not? Abel was a shepherd, and Cain was a farmer. Abel "brought of the firstborn of his flock and of their fat" (Genesis 4:4), burned them on the altar (see Leviticus 3:12–17), and offered them in faith (Hebrews 11:4, 6) to God. He also offered them cheerfully so his offering was accepted, for God loves a cheerful giver (2 Corinthians 9:6–7). His offering was accepted because he did the right thing in the absence of any written commandment, regulation, or precept, not because it was blood sacrifice. Cain's offering was not accepted because it was not the first of the firstfruits of his labor and it was given grudgingly, not because it was fruit of the ground.

Obviously Cain's offering was materially deficient because in Genesis 4:7 God said to him, "If you do well, will you not be accepted?" What was he to do for his offering to be accepted? The clue is in Exodus 34:26a, "*The first of the firstfruits of your land you shall bring to the house of the LORD your God*" (emphasis mine).

So if Cain had brought the first of the first fruits of his labor and offered it cheerfully with faith just as Abel did, his offering would have been accepted just as Abel's was. God is not a respecter of persons. He is a respecter of a person's deeds.

After Abel's death, when Adam was 130 years old (Genesis 5:3), he and Eve had another son they named Seth, meaning "anointed" or "compensation." (Adam and Eve were formed grown-up persons, but the age at which they had Cain and Abel has not been stated in the Scriptures.) Men began to proclaim the name of the Lord after Seth had a son he named Enosh (Genesis 4:26), meaning "man," in Hebrew. Adam lived for eight hundred years after they had Seth, and he and Eve had other sons and daughters (Genesis 5:4), and he died at the age of 930 years (Genesis 5:5).

Wait! Since there was probably no calendar at that time, how was Adam's age known precisely? Simple! In Genesis 1:14, we are told, "Then God said, 'Let there be lights in the firmament of the heavens to divide the day from the night; and let them be for signs and seasons, and for days and years.'" This means that from creation, among others, God created the seasons and made the moon, one of the lights, to mark them (Psalm 104:19).

People from the days of Adam, therefore, counted their age by the seasons. For example, if a person were born during the winter, he would be one year old during the next winter, which would come again in twelve months or moons and so on.

Adam and Eve's sons and daughters intermarried, and through them, the earth was filled with people in accordance with God's command in Genesis 1:28. It was one of Adam and Eve's daughters that Cain married after God banished him from His presence after killing his brother and went and lived in the land of Nod on the east of Eden (Genesis 4:16). Nod means "wondering." It is worthy of note that the Bible is not written in chronological order. (At that time, there was no law against one marrying one's close relative. That is why Father Abraham married his half-sister and it was perfectly all right in the sight of God.)

After King Abimelech of Gerar took Abraham's wife to marry her and God punished him and he wanted to know why he was not told the truth concerning the relationship between Abraham and Sarah, in explaining why Sarah said Abraham was her brother, Genesis 20:11–13 records,

> And Abraham said, "Because I thought, surely the fear of God *is* not in this place; and they will kill me on account of my wife. But indeed *she is* truly my sister. She *is* the daughter

of my father, but not the daughter of my mother; and she became my wife. And it came to pass, when God caused me to wander from my father's house, that I said to her, 'This *is* your kindness that you should do for me: in every place, wherever we go, say of me, 'He *is* my brother.''" (italics in the original).

Sarah was not Abraham's niece as some rabbis say of her.[1] She was his half-sister, as he himself said. They did not commit sexual sin because the law against incest was given many years afterward during the exodus (Leviticus 18:6–18, 20:11–21; Deuteronomy 27: 22). Unfortunately those rabbis are attempting to cover a sin that did not exist and to make Israeli culture look good in the eyes of unbelievers. God's laws are eternal, but apostle Paul writes in Romans 4:14–15, "For if those who are of the law *are* heirs, faith is made void and the promise made of no effect, because the law brings about wrath; for where there is no law *there is* no transgression" (italics in the original).

But in Acts 17:30–31 (NIV), it is written, "In the past God overlooked such ignorance, but now he commands all people everywhere to repent. For he has set a day when he will judge the world with justice by the man he has appointed. He has given proof of this to everyone by raising him from the dead."

Now God will not overlook any kind of sexual sin, no matter who commits it, because what amounts to sexual sin has been written down. It is common knowledge and should be known throughout the entire world. Ignorance of the law is no excuse.

As the population on earth exploded, wickedness grew to its zenith. And it was perfectly so because the murderer Cain built the first city on earth (Genesis 4:17) and Cain's offspring, Lamech, committed the second recorded murder in the Bible (Genesis 4:23). Lamech is also the first person named in the Bible to have had two wives, Adah and Zillah (Genesis 4:19). Lamech is also responsible for the Song of the Sword,

> Then Lamech said to his wives: "Adah and Zillah, hear my voice: Wives of Lamech, listen to my speech! For I have killed a man for wounding me, even a young man for hurting me. If Cain shall be avenged sevenfold, Then Lamech seventy-sevenfold." (Genesis 4:23–24)

Jesus Christ, however, taught that people must forgive others seventy times seven times (Matthew 18:22), and the Scriptures say vengeance belongs to God, not humankind (Romans 12:19). Lamech was of the sixth generation in Cain's line. So if the first city in the world were built by a murderer and one of his descendants was also a murderer and a polygamist, what moral behavior would the inhabitants of the city and subsequent ones exhibit?

Wickedness in the world got to the point that it grieved God's heart that He created human beings (Genesis 6:6), and so God set the maximum age of a person from then on to 120 years (Genesis 6:3). It is written that the thought of people and people's imagination was constantly filled with evil (Genesis 6:5), so after repeated warnings of impending destruction of humankind were ignored, God destroyed the world with floodwaters when Noah, one of Seth's offspring, was six hundred years old (Genesis 7:6). (Noah was of the eighth generation from Seth, and eight signifies a new beginning.)

Why were the warnings ignored? Until the flood of Noah, rain had never fallen on the earth. Water coming from beneath its surface watered the earth (Genesis 2:5–6). Therefore, because no rain had ever fallen from heaven, nobody believed that water could come from above to destroy the earth and almost everything therein. But at the appointed time, the waters underground erupted from the earth, and rain fell from heaven for forty days and forty nights to destroy everything on earth— man, woman, hermaphrodites, beast, bird, and everything that had breath in its nostrils, except Noah, his wife, his three sons, namely Shem, Ham, and Japheth and their three wives, as well as seven pairs (male and female) of every clean bird, animal, and all creeping things after their kind and two pairs (male and female) of every unclean bird, animal, and all creeping things after their kind to replenish the earth (Genesis 7). God saved them in an ark that He directed Noah to build. So Noah, his wife, and his three children and their wives, eight people in all, started human life on earth again after their ark landed "on the mountains of Ararat" (Genesis 8:4) in present-day Turkey.

When the Lord God formed Adam, He "planted a garden eastward in Eden; and there he put the man whom he had formed" (Genesis 2:8, 15). Adam and Eve lived in that beautiful garden called the garden of Eden. The garden was glamorous because God Himself planted it. A river flowed from it and divided into four riverheads, namely Pishon (the first head), Gihon (the second head), Hiddekel/Tigris (the third head), and Euphrates (the fourth head) (Genesis 2:10–14). The location of the Pishon River is described as skirting the entire land of Havilah where there is gold and the gold of that land is good. There is bdellium and also onyx stone there.

The location of the second river, Gihon, is said to be in the land of Cush (Ethiopia), and it goes around the whole land of Cush. The third and fourth rivers are also in the land of Cush. From the biblical narrative, it is obvious that the garden of Eden was located where the Black Sea is presently (see figure 1) (Genesis 2:8–14). The garden was probably swallowed up by the Black Sea when the earth was divided (see figure 3). Since Noah and his family lived through the destruction of almost everything that lived on the earth by the flood and knew the names of the original rivers and where they were, Ham, Noah's second son, named his first son Cush (Ethiopia), and Cush named his second son Havilah in order to identify the lands that were theirs from the beginning. They named their children after the original Cush and Havilah in Genesis 2:11–13, which help pinpoint the lands that the two rivers flowed around. Shem also had a Havilah in his offspring, but whereas Havilah in Cush's line is of the third generation after Noah, Havilah in Shem's line is of the sixth generation from Noah. Therefore, the lands mentioned in Genesis 2:11–13 were clearly inherited by the children of Ham. Not even one of the four river heads was wiped out or changed course during or immediately after the flood of Noah because the earth was not divided by then.

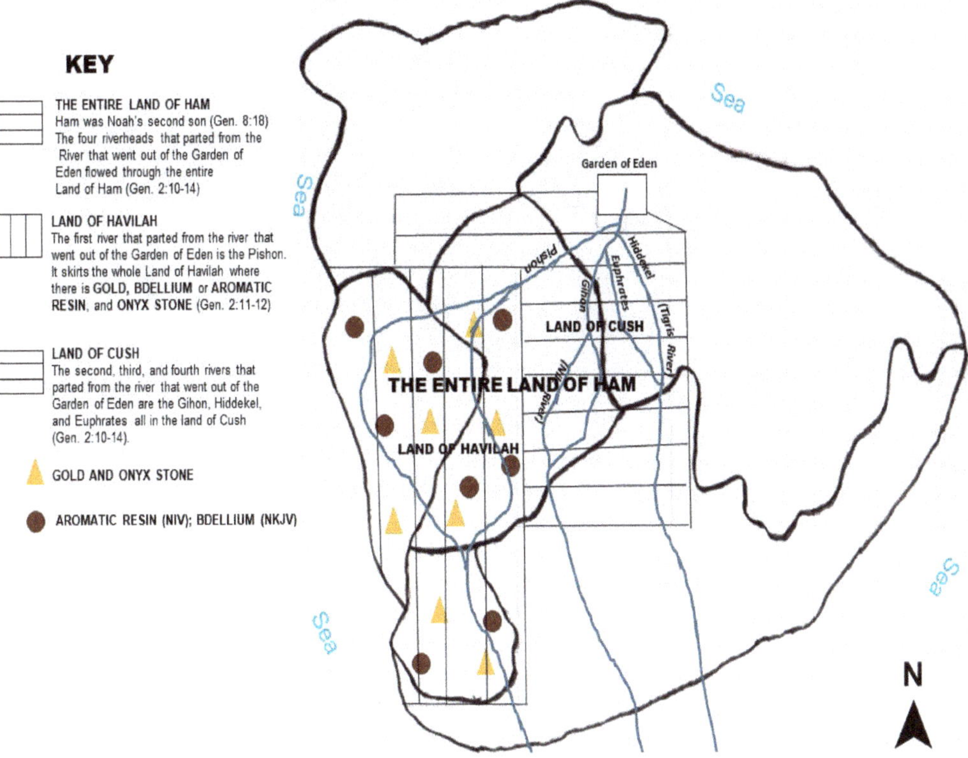

Figure 1: Sketch of the earth at creation showing the river that went out of the garden of Eden and its four heads (Genesis 2:8–14).

Because the flood destroyed all human beings except the eight people who were saved, in our era, the finding by scientists of the remains of dead people of ancient times grouped together may be construed by them and possibly others to mean that the earth was inhabited and later depopulated through death before the creation of Adam and Eve. Such interpretation begs the question: Whatever remains of dead people they find are simply the remains of the people who died during the flood of Noah and perhaps during other catastrophes thereafter.

Jesus Christ compared the days immediately preceding the day of His second coming to the days of Noah (Matthew 24:36–39), but how many people are paying attention to world events and the warnings and seek refuge in the boat, the church?

When God created the heavens and the earth, the universe was enveloped in water, and it was without form, but God said, "Let the waters under the heavens be gathered together into one place, and let the dry land appear; and it was so. And God called the dry land Earth, and the gathering together of the waters He called Seas: and God saw that it was good" (Genesis 1:9–10).

These verses tell us that at creation and before the flood of Noah and before the earth was divided, there was only one massive piece of land called earth or land and one mighty ocean called seas, as depicted in figure 2. Before God commanded the land to appear, He had created a firmament or an expanse, or canopy, between the waters above and the waters beneath to divide the waters above from the waters beneath (Genesis 1:7–9).

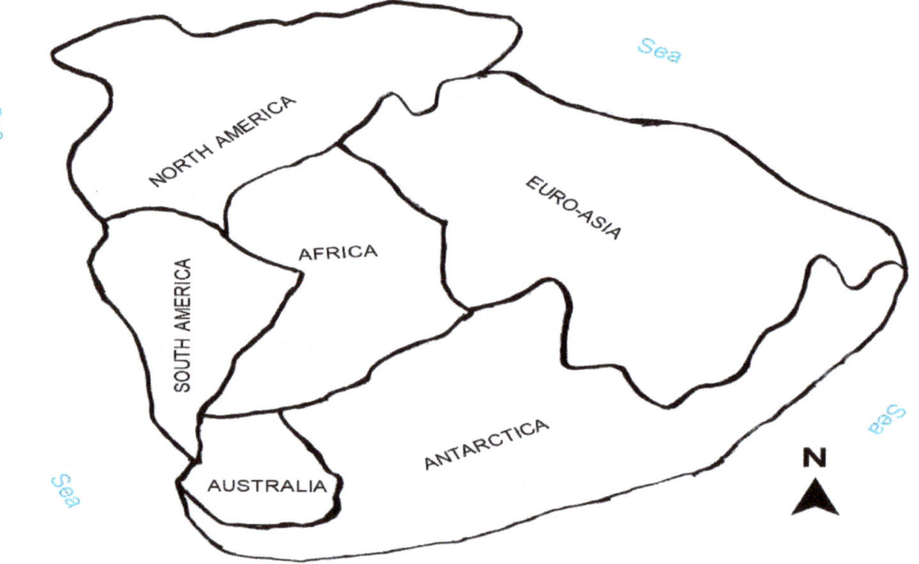

Figure 2: Sketch of the earth at creation (Genesis 1:9–10).

The firmament or expanse or canopy between the waters above and the waters beneath acted like the ozone layer that acts as a protective shield for life on earth. ("The ozone layer is one layer of the stratosphere, the second layer of the Earth's atmosphere. The stratosphere is the mass of protective gases clinging to our planet.")[19]

The firmament prevented the sun rays from hitting the earth hard, thereby creating a not-too-cool and not-too-hot balanced atmospheric conditions that supported unbelievably long life on earth.

In the case of Methuselah, it was almost a thousand years by man's reckoning! The balanced atmospheric conditions, coupled with human life that did not depend on the burning of fossil fuels that cause excessive carbon dioxide that traps heat near the surface of the earth, made the earth a heavenly place to live in.

But because the firmament above the earth was broken during the flood of Noah and the waters above fell on the earth, the water that came from beneath the earth to water ceased. And as the sun rays hit the earth, atmospheric conditions changed. The waters in the rivers and the seas heated, resulting in the waters evaporating. When the vapor reached a certain height, the heat dissipated, and the water condensed, forming a cloud. When the cloud became heavy, gravity pulled it down in the form of rain that watered the earth. The cycle repeats itself to this day.

This process, known as the hydrologic cycle and discovered by scientists in recent memory, actually commenced immediately after the flood of Noah in order for God to sustain human life again on the earth. The process is vividly described in the book of Job written many years ago,

> Behold, God *is* great, and we do not know *Him;* Nor can the number of His years *be* discovered. For He draws up drops of water, which distill as rain from the mist, Which the clouds drop down *and* pour abundantly on man. Indeed, can *anyone* understand the spreading of clouds, The thunder from His canopy? Look, He scatters His light upon it and covers the depths of the sea. For by these He judges the peoples; He gives food in abundance. (Job 36:26–31) (italics in the original)

The earth was divided after the flood of Noah.

CHAPTER 2

THE EMERGENCE OF MANY LANGUAGES AND THE DIVISION OF THE EARTH

Adam and Eve's descendants were numerous because they were fruitful, and they all spoke one language. Likewise, Noah's offspring were fruitful, and they all spoke one language, the same language spoken from the time of Adam until the understanding of their language was confused during the time of the building of the Tower of Babel (Genesis 11:7) led by Nimrod, a descendant of Ham through Cush, and they all lived together at one place.

After the flood, as the population started to increase, people began to move from the east around the mountains of Ararat where Noah's ark landed. As they moved, they found a plain in Shinar and settled there (Genesis 11:1–2). "And the whole earth was of one language, and of one speech. And it came to pass, as they journeyed from the east, that they found a plain in the land of Shinar; and they dwelt there" (KJV). Shinar is the same as Babel, Ur, Ur of the Chaldeans, Mesopotamia, and Babylon, which is present-day Iraq.

Under the leadership of Nimrod, the king of Mesopotamia, the people refused to obey God when He commanded them to spread and cover the whole earth and instead started to build a tower to the high heavens as a monument unto themselves, to make a name for themselves, and to serve as the seat of a one-world government. "Nimrod" means "rebellion." God, however, was not pleased with the people's rebelliousness and decided to confuse their language in order to stop the venture. The Holy Scriptures say,

> But the LORD came down to see the city and the tower the people were building. The LORD said, "If as one people speaking the same language they have begun to do this, then nothing they plan to do will be impossible for them. Come, let us go down and *confuse their language so they will not understand each other*." So the LORD scattered them from there over all the earth, and they stopped building the city.

That is why it was called Babel. There, the Lord confused the language of the whole world. "*From there the LORD scattered them over the face of the whole earth*" (Genesis 11:5–9 NIV) (emphasis mine).

God confused the understanding of their common words, not the words themselves. So when one person said a word, it meant something else to the hearer other than what it meant before. So the people dispersed and went away in groups according to the tongue they could understand, scattering all over the face of the earth. (That is why in etymology words can be traced to their origin). Thus, tribes, languages, and nations were formed. The tribes formed with their languages and tongues, were the tribes of Shem, Japheth, and Ham. (See figure 3.)

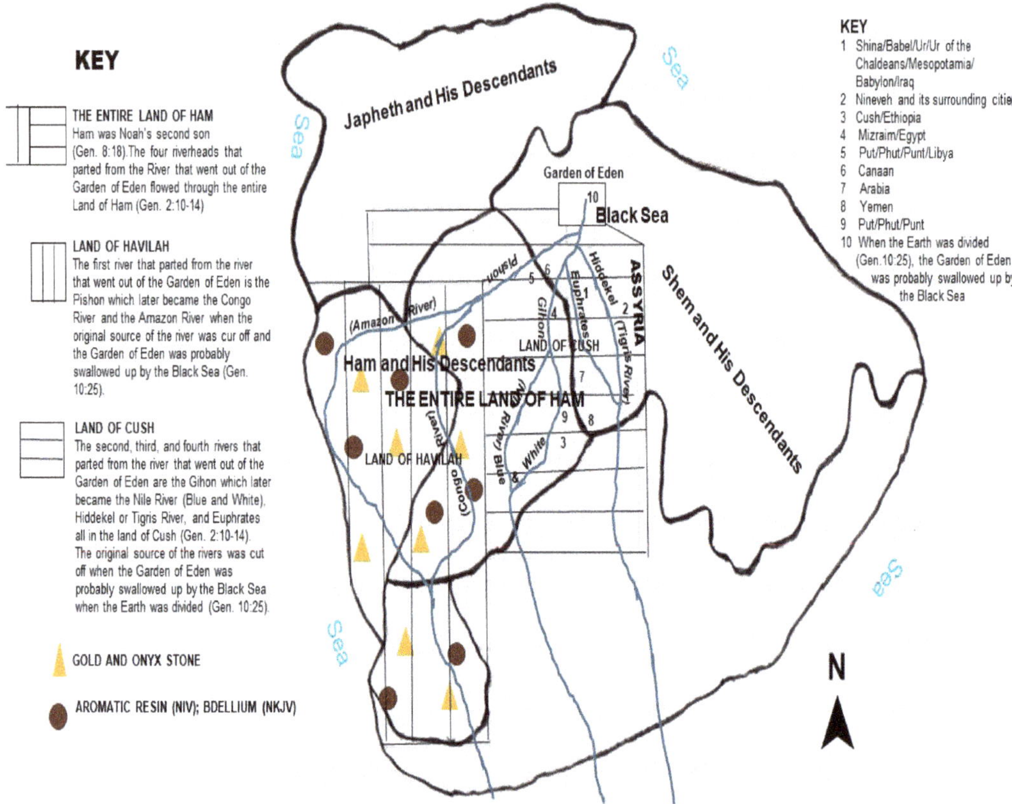

Figure 3: Political sketch of the world before the earth was divided.

They let off building the tower, and the place was called Babel, meaning "confusion." For this reason, if a nation becomes multi-language, they are not able to agree on anything they plan to do. In their Parliament, Senate, or House of Representatives, they speak Babel and never come to any understanding, much to the detriment of the nation.

The tower the people started to build, the Tower of Babel, was copied and later built in other parts of the world where human sacrifices were made during idol worship. It is known as Ziggurat, an artist's impression of which is shown below in figure 4.[39] Father Abraham migrated from Babel, also known as Ur or Ur of the Chaldeans and other names!

Figure 4: An artist's 3D reconstruction of the Great Ziggurat of Ur, based on a 1939 drawing by Leonard Woolley, *Ur Excavations*, volume V. The Ziggurat and its surroundings, Figure 1.4.

Human sacrifices were made at the very top of the Ziggurat.

When the person was killed, they were pushed down from the top of the Ziggurat and made to roll all the way down to the bottom, making sure that every drop of blood was squeezed from the person in order to appease the gods they believed caused the flood. This was the beginning of idol worship, and all people on earth practiced it.

Why were the gods to be appeased? Because of the canopy that God placed between the earth and the heavens, people on earth before the flood could not see the sun, moon, and stars in their glory and beauty. After the flood, however, the people for the first time saw the radiance and beauty of those heavenly bodies and assumed that those heavenly bodies caused the flood. So they had to worship and sacrifice to them in order to appease them and avert their wrath; otherwise they might again kill them with a flood.

When Nimrod supervised the building of the original Ziggurat, the intent, among others, was to keep the people from spreading all over the face of the earth as God commanded so he would become their king, but the subsequent Ziggurats that were built were purposefully for the worship of the sun, moon, or stars as god. As idol worship progressed, the worship went to the priest of the shrine instead of the god. The priest eventually became the king, then the representative of the god, and then the god that had to be worshipped.

As idol worship became common, during the days of Peleg, one of the descendants of Shem, the earth was divided most likely by an earthquake (Genesis 10:25; 1 Chronicles 1:19) into plates, as shown in figure 5.[23] Kingdoms, later becoming countries and states, emerged with their borders. "Peleg" means "division." He was of the fifth generation after Noah.

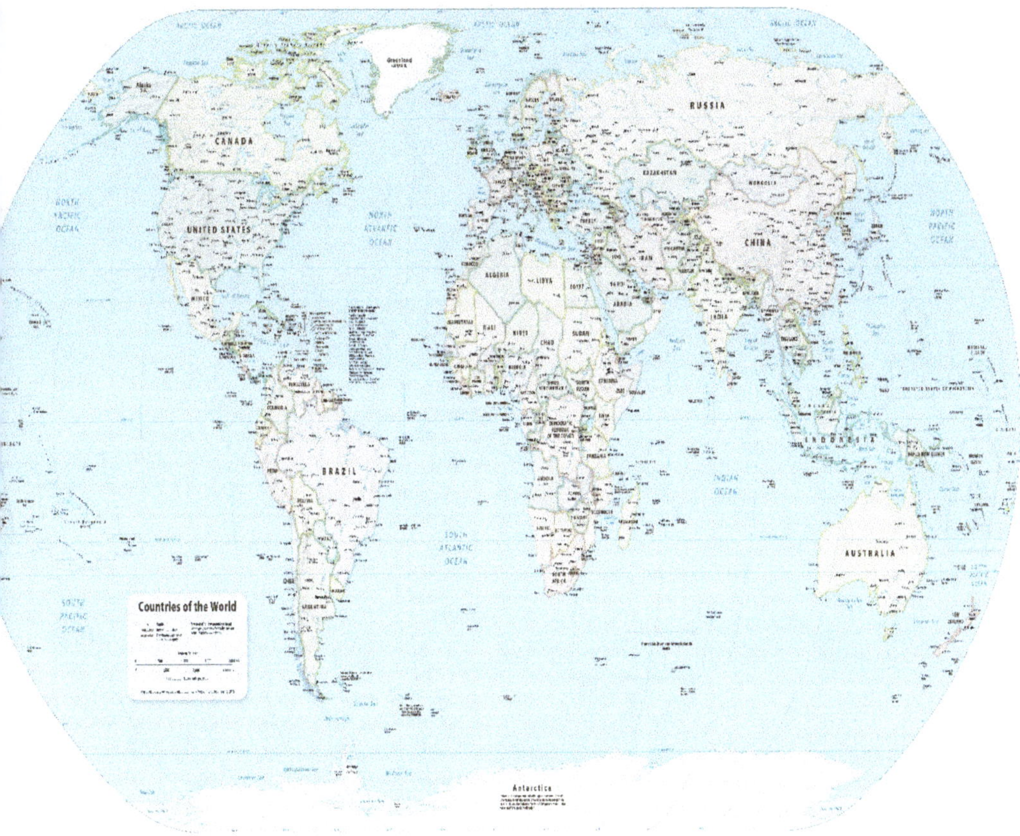

**Figure 5: Political map of the world today after the earth was divided
(Genesis 10:25; 1 Chronicles 1:19)**

If the earth were not divided, the political map of the world today would have looked like the map in figure 6.[26]

PANGEA POLITICA

Figure 6: An artist's impression of the political map of the world today had the earth not been divided (used by permission).

The earth was divided after the confusion of the understanding of the people's common words and after the formation of various tribes according to their new language. When the earth was divided, it happened that people who were living together and speaking the same language suddenly found themselves on a different plate or continent and completely lost contact with people on other plates for centuries and thought they were the only people on earth. That is why when continents like Africa and the Americas were "discovered" by the voyagers in the fifteenth century during the Age of Discovery, there were people on those continents when they were "discovered."

Some of the plates were, however, not completely severed from each other. They were joined by tiny strips of land, like the land that joined North Africa to the Middle East that made it possible for Father Abraham to journey from Ur right down to Egypt on foot or the back of a camel and also the land that joined South America to North America,[20] which enabled people to go from the Americas on foot and vice versa. Eastern Siberia and western Alaska were also joined together by a strip of land so people could go from one place to the other on foot. There was also no ice on the Antarctica, as portrayed by the Piri Reis Map of 1513, which Ian Harvey describes as a simple piece of preserved gazelle skin [that] has been the basis of intense controversy in the world of cartography. For one thing, the map appears to show Antarctica almost 300 years before it was discovered. Not only does it show Antarctica, but the continent is drawn as a land mass as it would have appeared before it was covered with its ice cap over 6,000 years ago.[14]

It is said,

Late in 1929, Gustav Deissmann, a German theologian, was working in Istanbul at the Topkapi Palace Library. While cataloging antique items he found a gazelle-skin parchment in a stack of discarded items. This parchment had a map drawn on it, and Deissmann was amazed to see that it appeared to show the outline of South America. He rescued the parchment, which is now known as the Piri Reis Map.[14]

So before the earth was divided, Antarctica was also part of the landmass as depicted in figure 2.

How long did it take the earth to divide into plates? According to the Holy Bible, which is inerrant in its original manuscripts, the earth was divided, as already stated, during the days of Peleg (Genesis 10:25). So how long were the days of Peleg on this earth? In Genesis 11:18–19, it is written, "Peleg lived thirty [30] years, and begot Reu. After he begot Reu, Peleg lived two hundred and nine years [209], and begot sons and daughters." Therefore, all the days of Peleg were 239 years, and he died. So if you are willing to believe, the earth was divided in a maximum of 239 years according to the Word of the Creator, not millions of geological years according to the word of man.

CHAPTER 3

SHEM AND HIS DESCENDANTS

Here are the descendants of Shem (Genesis 10:22–31). Shem had five sons, namely Elam, Ashur, Arphaxad, Lud, and Aram. The sons of A`ram were Uz, Hul, Gether, Meshek, and Mash.

The children of Arphaxad were Shelah, or Salah, and Shelah was the father of Eber. Eber had two sons, Peleg and Joktan. It was in the days of this Peleg that the earth was divided. Joktan had Almodad, Sheleph, Hazarmaveth, Jerah, Hadoram, Uzal, Diklah, Obal, Abimael, Sheba, Ophir, Havilah, and Jobab (Genesis 10:24–29).

Shem was the first son of Noah. At the time the language was confused at the Tower of Babel, it appears not all of Shem's and Japheth's descendants were there. The Canaanites, the descendants of Ham, were also not there. Therefore, after the dispersion, some of the Semites, descendants of Shem, and some of the Japhethites, descendants of Japheth, and the Canaanites still spoke the original language. This made it possible for Father Abraham to easily communicate with the inhabitants of Canaan when he sojourned in their land.

But what is the original language? Well, the original language is Hebrew, ancient Hebrew. Hebrew has been the spoken and written language from the time of Adam. This is firstly borne out by the fact that when Cain killed Abel, God put a mark on him, warning people that if anybody killed him in vengeance, vengeance would be taken on that person sevenfold (Genesis 4:14–15). If people could not write, read, and understand the written word, how were they able to read and understand the mark? But what did the mark look like? The mark was a stroke, or a series of strokes and squares, like in the original Hebrew alphabets.

Secondly, in Genesis 5:1, it is written, "This is the book of the genealogy of Adam …" Although it is believed and accepted that Moses wrote the first five books of the TaNaKh (the Jewish Holy Scriptures), called the Torah, he was actually handed a book, or record, of the creation story and the genealogy of Adam written in Hebrew, compiled right from the time of Adam, and passed on to the head of the family of each generation who added the events of their time until it got to him.

Moses added the events of his time, writing in the third person, and handed over the book to Aaron, the high priest. Joshua added the history of their time, and the book was handed over to succeeding high priests who added their stories. Then it was handed over to the head of families until it became the Holy Bible after the Redemption Story, in the form of the canonized books, was added and then handed over to the priests of the church and finally the entire world!

CHAPTER 4

JAPHETH AND HIS DESCENDANTS

Japheth was the youngest son of Noah. Here are his descendants as recorded in Genesis 10:2–5: Gomer, Magog, Madai, Javan, Tubal, Meshech, and Tiras. Gomer had Ashkenaz, Riphath, and Togarmah. Javan had Elishah, Tarshish, Kittim, and Dodamin.

When blessing his sons and descendants, Noah pronounced a blessing on Japheth that he would dwell in the tent of Shem, which means that Shem would cover Japheth and his descendants. Therefore, Japheth and his descendants operated in the shadows of Shem.

CHAPTER 5
HAM AND HIS DESCENDANTS

Ham was the second son of Noah. He had four sons: Cush, Mizraim, Put, and Canaan (Genesis 10:6). The other name of Cush is Ethiopia. The other name of Mizraim is Egypt. Put is the same as Libya, but Canaan has been called by the same name up to this day for easy identification purposes because it was Canaan, not Ham, who was cursed by Noah (Genesis 9:24–25). Canaan was one of the grandsons of Noah through Ham. The nations founded by the sons of Ham bear their names.

The Descendants of Cush (Kush) (or Ethiopia)

Cush, or Ethiopia, means "country of burnt faces" in Greek, and "Herodotus, the Greek historian, describes [the men of Ethiopia] as 'the tallest and handsomest of men.' They are frequently represented on Egyptian monuments, and they are all of the type of the true negro."[2] Therefore, a Cushite is a black person. Blacks played prominent roles in the history of the world and the church, as we are about to see.

The sons of Cush (or Ethiopia) were Seba, Havilah, Sabtah, Raamah, and Sabtecha. The sons of Raamah were Sheba, Dedan, and Nimrod (Genesis 10:7–8 KJV).

Seba and Sheba

What roles did the descendants of Seba and Sheba play in the history of the church? In Psalm 72:10ff (KJV) (a psalm written about Jesus Christ of Nazareth), it is written,

> The kings of Tarshish and of the isles shall bring presents: *the kings of Sheba and Seba shall offer gifts*. Yea, all kings shall fall down before him: all nations shall serve him … And he shall live, *and to him shall be given the gold of Sheba*: prayer also shall be made for him continually; and daily shall he be praised. (emphasis mine)

Some of the prophecies in Psalm 72 were fulfilled when Jesus Christ was born. It is written in Matthew 2:1–11 that wise men, or Magi or kings, came from the east to worship Him and brought Him gifts of gold, frankincense, and myrrh. Who were the wise men? According to tradition, they were Gaspar, Balthasar, and Melchior. They were descendants of Sheba and Seba, who were the descendants of Cush, the black man, and they fulfilled scripture.

Balthasar, also spelled Balthazar or Balthassa, was king of Arabia. He is venerated in the Roman Catholic Church, Eastern Orthodox Church, Anglican Communion, and Lutheran Church. "According to Western church tradition, Balthasar is often represented as a king of Arabia or sometimes Ethiopia and is thus frequently depicted as a Middle Eastern or Black man in art."[34] In fact, the original Arabs were blacks, and they inhabited Arabia and Yemen. We know this because before the earth was divided, Arabia and Yemen were part of present-day East Africa, as depicted in figure 3.

The Queen of Sheba

The Queen of Sheba is mentioned in 1 Kings 10:1–13 and 2 Chronicles 9:1–12. Though the Bible is silent on the name of the Queen of Sheba, it identifies her enough for later Jewish, Christian, and Islamic sources to identify her as "the beautiful Queen Makeda and the land of Sheba as ancient Ethiopia."[28]

The biblical account states that the Queen of Sheba visited King Solomon because she had heard great things about him and she came to verify things for herself. She was not disappointed. After Solomon satisfactorily answered all her questions and after seeing the beauty and quality of his living standard, she said to the king,

It was a true report which I heard in my land about your words and your wisdom. However I did not believe until I came and saw with my own eyes: and indeed the half was not told me. Your wisdom and prosperity exceed the fame of which I heard …" (1 Kings 10:6–7)

Before the queen returned to her homeland, she gave King Solomon great gifts of gold, rare spices, and precious stones. King Solomon also gave her great gifts, whatever she desired, besides what he was required to give her according to royal generosity. And King Solomon gave her something else too, a son!

According to Ethiopian history, the son, Menelik, who was born while the Queen of Sheba was on her way back to Ethiopia, ruled as king in Ethiopia, and his descendants also rule as kings in Ethiopia, tracing their kingdom to that of the Davidic monarchy in Israel. Also, according to the Ethiopians, when Menelik visited his father, King Solomon, when he was twenty-two years old, the king asked him to live in Israel and succeed him as king being his firstborn son, but he refused.

On his way back to Ethiopia, the king sent with him the ark of the covenant that Moses built, which is resting "within the Chapel of the Tablet next to the Church of Maryan in Aksuim, Ethiopia."[28] Though some scholars argue against the resting place of the ark in Ethiopia, no one has as yet proven where the ark of the covenant is.

Nimrod

Nimrod was the grandson of Cush and great-grandson of Ham, who was a son of Noah, and he built Ur, Nineveh, and other cities. Nineveh was the capital city of the Assyrian empire. Therefore, the Assyrians were blacks, or dark-skinned people.

"**Nineveh**, [was] the oldest and most-populous city of the ancient Assyrian empire, situated on the east bank of the Tigris River encircled by the modern city of Mosul, Iraq" (emphasis in the original).[17] Genesis 10:11 (NIV) buttresses the fact that Nimrod built Nineveh. Genesis 10:8–12 (NIV) thus states,

Cush was the father of Nimrod, who became a mighty warrior on the earth. He was a mighty hunter before the LORD; that is why it is said, "Like Nimrod, a mighty hunter before the LORD." The first centers of his kingdom were Babylon, Uruk, Akkad and Kalneh, in Shinar. From that land he went to Assyria, where he built Nineveh, Rehoboth Ir, Calah and Resen, which is between Nineveh and Calah—which is the great city.

So the original people of Babylon, Nineveh, and all the cities mentioned previously were black, or dark-skinned. Genesis 10:11 (KJV) states, however, "Out of that land went forth Asshur, and builded Nineveh, and the city Rehoboth, and Calah." Yet in the same version, it is written in Micah 5:6, "And they shall waste the land of Assyria with the sword, and the land of Nimrod in the entrances thereof: thus shall he deliver us from the Assyrian, when he cometh into our land, and when he treadeth within our borders," the implication here being that Ashur is the land of Assyria rather than the name of a person.

"Nimrod" stands for the Assyrians from whom Micah said they would be delivered. Nineveh was the city to which God sent Jonah to preach to its citizens to repent of their sins so God Himself would not destroy them, but Jonah refused and ran away in a ship. He was thrown into the sea and then swallowed by a whale and vomited on the shores of Nineveh. He then went and preached to the predominantly black people, and they repented of their sins and were saved. The word of God says,

> The Ninevites believed God. A fast was proclaimed, and all of them, from the greatest to the least, put on sackcloth. When Jonah's warning reached the king of Nineveh, he rose from his throne, took off his royal robes, covered himself with sackcloth and sat down in the dust. This is the proclamation he issued in Nineveh: "By the decree of the king and his nobles:
>
> Do not let people or animals, herds or flocks, taste anything; do not let them eat or drink. But let people and animals be covered with sackcloth. Let everyone call urgently on God.

> Let them give up their evil ways and their violence. Who knows? God may yet relent and with compassion turn from his fierce anger so that we will not perish." When God saw what they did and how they turned from their evil ways, he relented and did not bring on them the destruction he had threatened. (Jonah 3: 5–10 NIV)

So the black citizens of Nineveh knew, worshipped the God of heaven, the Creator, long ago, and obeyed Him when He sent a preacher to them to warn them of destruction if they did not repent of their sins.

As seen previously, when God commanded the people after the flood of Noah to scatter and fill the earth, Nimrod led a rebellion against God and set himself as king, earning the saying "Like Nimrod the mighty hunter before the LORD." It was Nimrod who probably started the worship of idols—the sun, the moon, and stars—after making himself king, thereby ensnaring the children of Noah in idol worship.

Idol worship is detestable to God because, among others, it is wrapped up in wickedness, and so He punishes such behavior seriously. Obviously Nimrod ensnared the Cushites in sin because when the children of Israel became pompous by reason of them being referred to as the chosen nation but were worshipping the idols of the surrounding nations, God said this of them, "Are not you Israelites the same to me as the Cushites? … Surely the eyes of the SOVEREIGN LORD are on the sinful kingdom. I will destroy it from the face of the earth. Yet I will not totally destroy the descendants of Jacob …" (Amos 9:7–8 NIV).

The KJV renders part of verse 7 as follows, "Are ye not as children of the Ethiopians unto me, O children of Israel?"

Why did God say such a thing about the Cushites or Ethiopians? It was because of their idol worship for which the children of Israel despised them yet did the same thing. In the first part of Jeremiah 13:23 (NIV), it is written, "Can the Ethiopian change his skin or a leopard its spots?" This is a metaphor that is interpreted in the second part of the verse, "Neither can you do good who are accustomed to doing evil." The Cushites—in fact all the people on earth before God called Abram (Father Abraham) from idol worship—were accustomed to doing evil in the sight of God by reason of their worship of the sun, the moon, and other gods, as was done in Egypt and in probably all the land of the Cushites. The Egyptians worshipped many gods, chief among them being the god Ra (Re) the sun god, which they thought was involved in creation and the afterlife. They knew the Creator God but did not worship Him.

However, after the Queen of Sheba visited King Solomon and returned, the lineage of her son that she had with the king began to worship the Creator God, the God of Israel, alone.

The Descendants of Mizraim (or Egypt)

Mizraim (KJV) or Egypt (NIV) was the second son of Ham. He had six sons: Ludim, Anamim, Lehabim, Naphtuhim, Pathrusim, and Casluhim (from whom came the Philistines and Caphtorim) (Genesis 10:13–14).

The Philistines

Israel was not the first chosen nation. The first chosen people were the Philistines and the Syrians. Amos 9:7 (NKJV) says,

> "Are you not like the people of Ethiopia to Me, O children of Israel?" says the LORD. "*Did I not bring up Israel from the land of Egypt, the Philistines from Caphtor and the Syrians from Kir*?" (emphasis mine)

This simple verse tells us that the Philistines and the Syrians were once upon a time chosen people whom the Lord delivered from Caphtor and Kir just as He delivered the children of Israel from Egypt but had to abandon them because of their sin. This is plain because the next verse (verse 8) says,

> "Behold, the eyes of the Lord GOD *are* on the sinful kingdom, And I will destroy it from the face of the earth; Yet I will not utterly destroy the house of Jacob," Says the LORD. (italics in the original)

The Descendants of Put (or Libya)

The descendants of Put/Phunt/Punt (or Libya) have not been listed in biblical records, but from Egyptian records, it is well known that they settled to the west of Egypt[6] in present- day Africa, in the country called Libya. Some, however, settled in the eastern part of Africa (see figure 3).

The Descendants of Canaan

Canaan, the fourth son of Ham, had Sidon, his firstborn. He was also the father, or ancestor, of the Hittites, Jebusites, Amorites, Girgashites, Hivites, Arkites, Arvadites, and Zemarites. In due time, the families of the Canaanites scattered. The border of the Canaanites was from Sidon, toward Gerar as far as Gaza, and then toward Sodom, Gomorrah, Admah, and Zeboyim, as far as Lasha (Genesis 10:15–19).

Jerusalem was a Jebusites city. Here are the biblical records,

> And the border went up by the Valley of the Son of Hinnom to the southern slope of the *Jebusite city (which is Jerusalem)*; *As for the Jebusites, the inhabitants of Jerusalem*, the children of Judah could not drive them out; *but the Jebusites dwell with the children of Judah at Jerusalem to this day*. (Joshua 15: 8, 63) (emphasis mine)

> The king [David] and his men marched to *Jerusalem* to attack the *Jebusites, who lived there*. The Jebusites said to David, "You will not get in here; even the blind and the lame can ward you off." They thought, "David cannot get in here." Nevertheless, David captured the fortress of Zion—which is the City of David. On that day David had said, "Anyone who conquers the Jebusites will have to use the water shaft to reach those 'lame and blind' who are David's enemies." That is why they say, "The 'blind and lame' will not enter the palace." David then took up residence in the fortress and called it the City of David. He built up the area around it, from the terraces inward. And he became more and more

powerful, because the LORD God Almighty was with him. (2 Samuel 5:6–10 NIV) (emphasis mine)

Though David conquered the city, there is no record that he killed everyone. Therefore, the Jebusites (blacks, or dark-skinned people) lived with the people of Judah and eventually became part of the tribe of Judah. Two of the kings of the Jebusites were Melchizedek, king of Salem (Jeru- salem) who blessed Father Abraham (Genesis 14:17–20), and Adoni-Zedek, king of Jerusalem (Joshua 10:1–5). So the people from whom Israel took the land were blacks, children of Ham. But from the time of the conquest of the land of Canaan during the exodus, Jerusalem could not be conquered until the time of King David. (Jeru means "city," Salem means "peace," and Jerusalem means "city of peace." Melchizedek means "King of righteousness," and Adoni-Zedek means "Lord of righteousness.") Jesus Christ is priest forever in the order of Melchizedek (see Psalm 110:4 and Hebrews 7:17).

In the Genesis account concerning Noah, his drunkenness, and what happened afterward, it is written that after Noah woke up from his drunkenness, he discovered that he had been violated. The Holy Scriptures state that Ham, his younger son (NKJV), saw his nakedness and told his brothers, so Noah cursed Canaan. Genesis 9:24–27 NIV)[7] says,

> When Noah awoke from his wine and found out what his *youngest* son had *done* to him, he said, "*Cursed be Canaan!* The lowest of slaves will he be to his brothers." He also said, "Praise be to the LORD, the God of Shem! May Canaan be the slave of Shem. May God extend Japheth's territory; may Japheth live in the tents of Shem, and may Canaan be the slave of Japheth." (emphasis mine)

Ham was the younger son of Noah, not the youngest. Noah had three sons: Shem, Ham, and Japheth. So why was Ham described as the youngest son? If Noah cursed his youngest son, who happened to be Japheth, but the Scriptures say he actually blessed Japheth, then who saw Noah's nakedness? And why was Canaan cursed if it were Ham who saw Noah's nakedness? Was it really Ham who saw Noah's nakedness? And what does seeing a person's nakedness mean? The Scriptures say, "When Noah awoke from his wine and found out what his youngest son had *done* to him ..." What did his youngest son do to him?

In Leviticus 18:7, it is written, "The *nakedness of your father* or the nakedness of your mother *you shall not uncover ...*" (emphasis mine). The Modern English Version (MEV) renders the verse as follows, "*You shall not have relations with your father* or have relations with your mother ..." (emphasis mine), and in Leviticus 18:6 (NIV), it is written, "*No one is to approach any close relative to have sexual relations. I am the LORD*" (emphasis mine).

What do these laws mean? They mean exactly what they say: that a person should not have sex with his father, mother, or any close relative. So when Scripture said Ham saw Noah's nakedness, what actually happened? What happened was that Canaan, the grandson of Noah through Ham, had anal sex with Noah when he was intoxicated. That was what Canaan had done to Noah: he sodomized him! And Noah cursed him.

The curse was so effective that the Canaanites became homosexuals. Seeing a person's nakedness is the same as uncovering the person's nakedness and the same as having sex with the person as afore written. The Scriptures say that Ham saw Noah's nakedness because he was the father of the generations after him and therefore was responsible for their behavior and required to teach them the things of God, having seen the wrath of God firsthand. Noah, however, cursed the actual person who committed the crime. The narrative that Ham was the youngest son of Noah is because Canaan was Noah's grandson and Ham, in this case, stands for his posterity. (Noah lived 350 years after the flood [Genesis 9:28], long enough for his grandchildren to be his contemporaries.)

When God delivered the Hebrews from Egypt, because of the curse on Canaan and mainly because the cup of the Canaanites was full with sin, He gave them the land that originally belonged to Canaan and his descendants, setting their borders from the Red Sea to the Mediterranean Sea (in Hebrew, the Sea of the Philistines) and from the desert to the Euphrates River (Exodus 23:31). The land is mentioned as belonging to the Canaanites, Hittites, Amorites, Perizzites, Hivites, and Jebusites, a land flowing with milk and honey (Exodus 3:17), as well as the land of the Girgashites and the dispersed families of the Canaanites as far as Gaza toward Sodom and Gomorrah, Admah and Zeboiim, and as far as Lasha (Genesis 10:15–20). The homosexual capitals of Canaan were Sodom and Gomorrah until God destroyed those two cities and all the cities of the plain near them with brimstone and fire (Genesis 19:12–29). Furthermore, during the exodus, Joshua made slaves of the Gibeonites, who were Hivites (Joshua 9) in fulfillment of Noah's curse on Canaan.

Canaan forfeited his inheritance to the children of Shem and Japheth because of gay sex just as Esau sold his birthright to Jacob for some red stuff (Genesis 25:29–34). When Esau was crying bitterly for some leftover blessing after Jacob had been blessed, Genesis 27:39–40 (ESV) states,

> Then Isaac his father answered and said to him: "Behold, away from the fatness of the earth shall your dwelling be, and away from the dew of heaven on high. By your sword you shall live, and you shall serve your brother; but when you grow restless you shall break his yoke from your neck."

The key words here are "when you grow restless you shall break his yoke from your neck." When the children of Canaan grew restless from the yoke of slavery and servitude to the children of Shem and Japheth as a result of the curse, they tried through conflict between them and Israel to free themselves but were unsuccessful. However, I, Emmanuel Kofi Bonney, at the direction of Jesus Christ of Nazareth and by the power of the Holy Spirit, broke the curse after the fifty-day war between Israel and Gaza in 2014.

Because the curse had been broken, when Israel Defense Minister Lieberman refused to accept the cease-fire, ending two days of fighting with the militants in Gaza in 2018, and wanted to continue fighting and completely destroy them but could not get his way, he had to resign. There was actually nothing to fight for again so God had to put him aside. He could not read the signs of the time.

Israel and the Canaanites are not going to fight a liberation war again. The yoke has been broken in the name of Jesus Christ of Nazareth! If they ever fight a war again, it will not be for liberation from slavery and servitude to the children of Shem and Japheth. It will be a misguided adventure, or a fight, as a result of a pure desire for supremacy or a religious war that will culminate in the final battle of Armageddon, which will engulf the entire world and end with those opposing God being permanently vanquished.

CHAPTER 6

FATHER ABRAHAM AND OTHERS IN THE LAND OF THE BLACKS

During biblical times, present-day Africa was sometimes called Egypt, Ethiopia, the Land of Cush, or the Land of Ham. Egypt and Ethiopia therefore stood for the countries that bear their name and also the entire region of Africa. Africa, Africans, and blacks played very important roles in the formation of the church, as seen previously and as follows.

Among the significant people who went to Africa for solace and protection and events that happened during the revelation of the church in the wilderness and the church birthed by Jesus Christ of Nazareth on the cross when His side was pierced and water and blood flowed out of Him are as follows:

❖ **Father Abraham**

- When Father Abraham was called from Ur of the Chaldeans built by Nimrod, the son of Cush, and he and his wife Sarah and others walked through the land that God promised him and his descendants, he ended up in Egypt because of a famine in the land where he sojourned (Genesis 12:10–20).

- The Egyptians took good care of him and his family, and the king of Egypt (Pharaoh) gave him male and female servants, sheep, oxen, male donkeys, female donkeys, and camels.

- Among the female servants that Pharaoh gave Sarah was Hagar, who later became Abraham's concubine.

- The male and female servants that Pharaoh gave Abraham were black, or dark-skinned people. Therefore, a majority of Abraham's household was made of blacks, or dark- skinned people.

- Egypt fed the entire then world during the famine.

❖ Keturah, Wife of Father Abraham

Father Abraham married Keturah, a Cushite (or an Ethiopian) after the death of Sarah, his wife (Genesis 25:1 KJV), and God was pleased with it. The verse reads, *"Abraham had taken another wife, whose name was Keturah"* (emphasis mine). Note that Keturah was Father Abraham's wife, not his concubine. Keturah was a black woman. Abraham had six sons with her: Zimran, Jokshan, Medan, Midian, Ishbak, and Shuah (Genesis 25:2 KJV).

There is no record in the Scriptures that Abraham sent the sons of Keturah away from Isaac. Genesis 25:6 (KJV) reads, "But unto the sons of the *concubines*, which Abraham had, Abraham gave gifts, and sent them away from Isaac his son, while he yet lived, eastward, unto the east country" (emphasis mine). This means that Father Abraham had two wives, Sarah and Keturah, and also had concubines with whom he had other sons. The names, nationalities, and skin color of the concubines and the names of their children have not been stated in the Scriptures. The Scriptures, however, state categorically clear that Father Abraham had concubines besides his wives, Sarah and Keturah, but it is the names of Abraham's wives, Sarah and Keturah; *one concubine*, Hagar; and the names of their children only that have been stated in the Scriptures. Abraham married a black woman because God never told him not to marry a black woman or anyone not from his tribe; at least there is no record that He did or did not when he married Keturah or afterward. Abraham told his servant, the head of his household, not to get a Canaanite wife for his son Isaac (Genesis 24:3) because the Canaanites had been cursed and also not to send Isaac back to where he came from because he had been called out of idolatry and would not like his son to go back to his vomit. During the time of the exodus,

God told those who were on the way to the Promised Land not to intermarry with those they were going to dispossess of their inheritance. In Deuteronomy 7:1–4 (NIV), God listed the specific people groups that those that He had redeemed from Egypt should not intermarry with. Here are the relevant verses,

> When the LORD your God brings you into the land you are entering to possess and drives out before you many nations— the Hittites, Girgashites, Amorites, Canaanites, Perizzites, Hivites and Jebusites, seven nations larger and stronger than you— and when the LORD your God has delivered them over to you and you have defeated them, then you must destroy them totally. Make no treaty with them, and show them no mercy. Do not intermarry with them. Do not give your daughters to their sons or take their daughters for your sons, for they will turn your children away from following me to serve other gods, and the LORD's anger will burn against you and will quickly destroy you.

So one of the reasons why God instructed the redeemed not to intermarry with the aforementioned people was that they would lead them into idolatry. It was not because of their skin color. Besides that, God listed the specific people groups that the redeemed should not intermarry with.

❖ Hagar, Father Abraham's Concubine

When Father Abraham was sojourning in the land of Palestine and ended up in Egypt because of the severe famine mentioned previously and his wife, Sarah, was taken from him to marry the king of Egypt because she told the people he was her brother, God was not pleased with the situation Abraham found himself in and punished the household of the king. When the king learned the truth that Sarah was Abraham's wife, he let Sarah go and allowed Abraham to leave with all the gifts and servants he had given him on account of Sarah. As stated previously, among the female servants was Hagar, an Egyptian, a black, or dark-skinned woman. Egypt was one of the sons of Ham, as we have already seen. The Egyptians before, during, and after Old Testament times, but before the invasion of other people groups and the Muslim conquest in 639 or 640 AD were black, or dark-skinned. This is borne out by the numerous Egyptian mummies unearthed over the years. Cheikh Anta Diop (1923–1986), a Senegalese scholar, also argues, "ancient Egypt was built, ruled, and populated by dark-skinned African people."[33] Diop found that even after hundreds of years of intermixing with foreign invaders, the blood type of modern Egyptians is the "same group B as the populations of Western Africa on the Atlantic seaboard and not the A2 group characteristic of the white race prior to any crossbreeding."[33]

Also King Tutankhamun (pronounced Tutankhamen) c.1342–c.1325 BC, an ancient Egyptian king who was exhumed and unmasked, was a completely black person. One could tell by his teeth, nose, and the contours of his face. But the golden mask that covered his face has been paraded throughout parts of the world portraying him as if he were from a different ethnic group. There is also an artist's imaginary presentation of his face being circulated in the media to prove that he was not black. All these amount to distortion of historical facts.

❖ **Ishmael, Son of Hagar**

Hagar bore Father Abraham a son whom he named Ishmael. Ishmael was therefore a black man. God told Abraham that He had blessed Ishmael and that He "will make him fruitful, and will multiply him exceedingly. He shall beget twelve princes, and I will make him a great nation" (Genesis 17:20–21 KJV). God also said of him, "He will be a wild donkey of a man; his hand will be against everyone and everyone's hand against him, and he will live in hostility toward all his brothers" (Genesis 16:12 NIV). The Islamic religion traces its root to Ishmael.

❖ **Joseph**

Joseph, one of the twelve sons of Jacob, was sold into slavery to Potiphar in Egypt (Genesis 39) by his elder brothers because of jealousy. First, his brothers wanted to sell him to Ishmaelites (the descendants of Ishmael) but ended up selling him to Midianites (descendants of Midian, one of Father Abraham and Keturah's sons). After being falsely accused of rape by his master's wife, Joseph landed in prison, where he interpreted the dreams of two other prisoners, which came to pass. A while after, the king of Egypt had a dream, but his magicians, wise men, and astrologers could not interpret it for him. Joseph, on the recommendation of the king's cupbearer who was one of the prisoners whose dream Joseph interpreted, was brought from prison to interpret the king's dream. After he successfully interpreted the dream, the king changed his name to Zaphenath-Paneah, made him second-in-command after him in the whole land of Egypt, and gave him an Egyptian wife, Asenath, who was the daughter of Potiphera, the priest of On. Once again, Egypt fed the entire then world under the direction and management capabilities of Joseph during a severe famine that lasted seven years (Genesis 39–41).

❖ **Asenath, Wife of Joseph**

Joseph had two sons with Asenath (Genesis 46:27), the black, or dark-skinned, woman. Their names were Manasseh and Ephraim (Genesis 46:20).

Manasseh and Ephraim

No Hebrew tribe bears the name of Joseph, and Benjamin, Joseph's brother from the same mother, Rachel, was also assimilated into the tribe of Judah. So to have twelve tribes, Manasseh and Ephraim became two distinct tribes. Therefore, two tribes of Israel, Manasseh and Ephraim, are blacks because they are descendants of a black woman.

In determining race, not nationality, a person is classified a black if one of the person's parents is black, as in the case of former President Barack Hussein Obama of the United States of America, who is classified a black because he had a black father from Kenya in East Africa and a white mother from Kansas, United States. Meghan Markle, Duchess of Sussex and wife of Prince Harry of the United Kingdom, has a black mother and a white father, both U.S. citizens, but is classified black because of her black mother.

❖ Jacob and His Entourage

Jacob, Joseph's father, who is also called Israel, and his entourage of sixty-nine people, seventy people in all, were taken care of by the Egyptians when they migrated to Egypt during the seven years of famine that engulfed the world at that time. They were given food and shelter as well as the best part of the land (Goshen) that suited their occupation. They lived peacefully in Egypt and multiplied greatly in numbers until the events that led to the exodus (Genesis 46:1–26; Exodus 1:8ff).

❖ Joshua

Joshua, son of Nun, who was Moses' assistant and leader of the tribes of Israel after Moses' death, was from the tribe of Ephraim and a descendant from the union between Joseph and Asenath (Numbers 13:8). Therefore, he was a black man.

❖ Moses

- Moses, who eventually delivered the Hebrews from Egypt, was saved from death by the daughter of the Egyptian king (Exodus 2:1–10).

- Moses lived in the palace of the Egyptian king, was treated as the king's son, and was fully educated as an Egyptian prince.

❖ Jethro, the Priest of Midian and Moses' Father-in-Law

The priest of Median, Jethro, also called Reuel (Exodus 2:16, 18) was a black man. It was one of his seven daughters, Zipporah, that Moses married after he ran away from Pharaoh, the king of Egypt, after he had killed an Egyptian and the king sought to kill him (Exodus 2:11–15). Jethro was a descendant of Midian, one of the six sons Keturah bore Father Abraham.

❖ Zipporah, Wife of Moses

Zipporah was a black woman, a Cushite or Ethiopian. In Numbers 12:1 (KJV), it is written, "And Miriam and Aaron spake against Moses because of the *Ethiopian woman whom he had married:*

for he had married an Ethiopian woman" (emphasis mine). Now if Zipporah were an Ethiopian or a Cushite (NIV), then it necessarily follows that her father, Jethro/Ruel, the priest of Median, was a black man descended from Midian who descended from Keturah, Abraham's black wife. So it was in a black man's home that the man of God, Moses, found respite when he was running away from danger. And it was in a black woman's bosom that he found comfort and security. Moses had two sons with Zipporah: Gershom (Exodus 2:22) and Eliezer (Exodus 18:4).

Gershom and Eliezer

Gershom and Eliezer, Moses' sons, were blacks because their mother was black. They were absorbed into the Levite tribe of the Hebrews. This is what is said about them in 1 Chronicles 23:14 (NIV), "The sons of Moses the man of God were counted as part of the tribe of Levi." The Levites were the priests of the Most High God.

Gershom

Though nothing is said about Gershom himself in the Scriptures, it is stated in Judges 18:30–31 that his son, Jonathan, also known as Shebuel according to the Targum, became an apostate priest. It was he who led the Danites in idol worship. This is what the above-quoted scriptures (NIV) say, "There the Danites set up for themselves the idol, and Jonathan son of Gershom, the son of Moses[2] and his sons were priests for the tribe of Dan until the time of the captivity of the land. They continued to use the idol Micah had made, all the time the house of God was in Shiloh."

Eliezer

The Scriptures do not say anything about Eliezer himself, but his offspring did not become idolaters like those of his elder brother, Gershom. It is written in the Scriptures that Eliezer had one son called Rehabiah, but Rehabiah's sons are very numerous

---

[2] Some translations, including the New King James Version, identify Gershom as son of Manasseh.

(1 Chronicles 23:17), and they faithfully served the Lord God Almighty.

❖ Jeroboam

When King Solomon sought to kill Jeroboam because God told him that He would tear away the kingdom from him and give it to his servant because "his heart was turned away from the Lord" (1 Kings 11:5–13), Jeroboam fled to Shishak, king of Egypt, and stayed there until the death of Solomon (1 Kings 11:40–41). Once again, Egypt gave protection to a man chosen by God.

When the chosen people of God are about to perish, God uses blacks to rescue them.

CHAPTER 7

THE MIXED MULTITUDE

Are there black Hebrews and, therefore, black Israelites? The answer to this question is a resounding, "Yes, there are." Prior to the children of Israel leaving Egypt and taking possession of the Promised Land, there was no nation on earth called Israel; there was only one man called Israel.

When God delivered Father Abraham's descendants from Egypt after the tenth plague in which the firstborn of Pharaoh and the firstborn of every man and animal died as described in Exodus 12:29–33, many other people went out of Egypt with them. The people that left with them are described as a mixed multitude (Exodus 12:38 KJV). Who were the "mixed multitude"? They were people of different skin colors and probably of different mother tongues even though they all might have spoken Hebrew as a *lingua franca*. Among them were probably mostly Egyptian blacks who saw the wonders of Yahweh, the God of the Hebrews, as opposed to the powers of the Egyptian gods, and went away with the children of Israel.

On reaching the Promised Land, they settled under the flags of the twelve tribes of the twelve sons of Jacob who was renamed Israel by God, as recorded in Genesis 32:22–32. The people that comprised the confederacy of the twelve tribes of Israel were called Hebrews. Hebrew means "cross over," and Father Abraham was the first person to be referred to as Abram the Hebrew when he and his men defeated the kings that took Lot, his family, and his possessions away in a raid (Genesis 14:13).

Probably Abram was so called because he crossed over from Ur to the land of Canaan, which the accursed people of the land inhabited. Maybe other people groups shunned the Canaanites because of their accursed identity, so Abram crossing over the border to come to them was a thing of awe.

Hebrew was also the language that Abraham spoke. Once in the Promised Land, every one of whatever skin color who wanted to be absorbed into the clans of the Hebrews was so absorbed and became a Hebrew. Their inclusion in the Hebrew tribes is in accordance with what Yahweh had decreed as recorded in Exodus 12:48–50.

> *"And when a stranger dwells with you and wants to keep the Passover to the LORD, let all his males be circumcised, and then let him come near and keep it; and he shall be as a native of the land.* For no uncircumcised person shall eat it. One law shall be for the native-born and for the stranger who dwells among you." Thus all the children of Israel did; as the LORD commanded Moses and Aaron, so they did. (emphasis mine)

Besides that, during the years that the Hebrews lived in Egypt, apart from those we have already noted married blacks, they surely intermarried with people from other people groups. The offspring from such marriages also probably left Egypt during the exodus. The intermarriages were perfect because there was no law prior to their leaving Egypt that the Hebrews should not marry from other tribes (see above). In any case, as we have seen previously, the Jebusites, who are blacks, were the original owners of Jerusalem and live there up to this day.

CHAPTER 8

JESUS AND THE MODERN CHURCH IN THE LAND OF THE BLACKS AND OTHER PROMINENT BLACKS IN THE ANNALS OF CHURCH HISTORY

The church, as we have seen at the beginning, began when God proclaimed the first gospel (Protoevangelium). Throughout the ages, the church has marched forward unhindered with blacks, Cushites, or Ethiopians and the land of Cush (Africa) playing major roles in its forward march. At the fullness of time, the seed of the woman was born without the involvement of a man. But as prophesied in Hosea 11:1, Jesus Christ of Nazareth, the Savior of the world, found Himself in Egypt.

Jesus Christ of Nazareth, the Savior of the World, in Egypt

In Jeramiah 31:15, it is written, "Thus says the LORD: 'A voice was heard in Ramah, Lamentation and bitter weeping, Rachel weeping for her children, Refusing to be comforted for her children, Because they are no more.'"

In Saint Matthew's account of the birth of Jesus Christ and its aftermath, he narrates the murder of children two years and below ordered by King Herod (a Roman) in his attempt to kill Jesus and cites the above prophecy as having been fulfilled by Herod. He says in Matthew 2 that when Jesus was born, the wise men who saw His star in the east and came to worship Him inquired of His birthplace in Jerusalem, and they were told He was born in Bethlehem. When departing to Bethlehem, King Herod asked them to come back and report the location of Jesus to him so he would also go and worship Him, but he actually planned to have Him killed.

Having been warned by the omniscient God of Herod's plan, the wise men did not come back to report to him. So Herod, overcome by hatred, jealously, and insecurity, ordered the murder of all Jewish male offspring two years and below because he figured out that from what the Magi had told him that Jesus would have been up to about two years old at the time. But before Herod could put his diabolical plan into action, God had warned Joseph, the guardian of Jesus, in a dream and told him to escape with his family to Egypt so it would be fulfilled the prophecy, *"Out of Egypt I called my son"* (Matthew 2:14–15; Hosea 11:1)(emphasis mine). So to Egypt they fled.

Therefore, it was in the land of Egypt that Jesus's life was saved. They stayed in Egypt until Herod's death before returning to Nazareth after Joseph was told in a dream that those who sought to take the child's life were dead. Previously we have seen that the wise men gave Jesus gifts of gold, frankincense, and myrrh. Why did they give Him such gifts? Origen of Contra Celsum, interpreted the gifts as having spiritual meaning: the gold symbolized Jesus' kingship and authority on earth as well as His divine kingship and authority; the frankincense symbolized His deity; and the myrrh symbolized His mortality and death. Other schools of thought have given various reasons why Jesus was given those gifts, such as that the gold symbolized virtue; the frankincense symbolized prayer; and the myrrh was for His suffering or burial. But apart from the symbolism of the gifts, what were they actually meant for? Was the myrrh used for His burial as those other schools of thought taught? When Jesus died, Mary did not provide any myrrh for His burial; neither did Jesus tell His disciples that He had some myrrh hidden anywhere that they could use to prepare His body for burial when He told them about His impending death (Matthew 16:21–28). Therefore, the myrrh could not be meant for His burial. Joseph of Arimathea provided the linen shroud for Jesus's burial (Matthew 27:57–60). And after His burial, on the third day, women, including Mary Magdalene, bought spices to go and anoint His body (Mark 16:1).

So what were the gifts meant for? They were to be sold and the proceeds used to take care of Jesus, Mary, and Joseph. Since Joseph and his family had to flee to Egypt, they obviously had not made provision for their living expenses there. But God had! So when they were in Egypt, they sold the myrrh and other items to take care of themselves; hence neither Mary nor Joseph provided anything for Jesus's burial.

At that time, Egypt was the greatest nation on earth, and the Egyptians were seriously into embalming their dead. Therefore, the myrrh and frankincense, which are used in burial rites and for embalming dead bodies, fetched them really good money. Likewise, the gold, which was used to make ornaments and face masks for their dead Pharaohs and even buried with their kings and nobles, fetched good money. Frankincense and myrrh were also used in their idol worship.

Egypt, the Cradle of the Infant Church

Egypt was the cradle of the church during its infancy. Alexandria in Egypt was where Christian theology was shaped. Among the theologians in Egypt were:

Athanasius the Great (296–373 AD)

- Athanasius' enemies gave him the nickname "Black Dwarf" because he was a short, dark-skinned Egyptian bishop.[10]

- He successfully challenged the heresy of "Arius [A.D. 256–336], a presbyter (priest) from *Libya* who announced, 'If the Father begat the Son, then he who was begotten had a beginning in existence, and from this it follows there was a time when the Son was not.'"[11] Athanasius and Alexander, the bishop of Alexandria in Egypt, fought against Arius' assertion, arguing that it denied the Trinity because Jesus Christ is of the same essence as God (Homoousios), not of like essence (Homoiousia). This is because salvation was at stake; if Jesus were not the same as God, then he could not atone for human sin since it is only the person who is fully God and fully man can save. A creature—a created being—like all other creations of God cannot atone for human sin.

Therefore, Arius' interpretation of Scripture was simply deductive reasoning, or deductive logic, or human philosophy and therefore vain. Paul warned against vain philosophy (Colossians 2:8). In fact, philosophical perception of God leads to theological misconception of the true nature and deity of God.

- Arius was excommunicated from the church at a synod in Alexandria in September 323 AD, but he was sheltered by Eusebius of Nicomedia, who sponsored a synod in October 323 AD to nullify Arius' excommunication. Eusebius sided with Arius and refused to accept Jesus Christ as being of the same essence as the Father.[35] But here is the crux of the matter: Any religion or sect that denies the deity of Jesus Christ and teaches that Jesus Christ was a created being and therefore just a god has seriously missed the basic salvation plan.

- Athanasius helped craft the Nicene Creed, one of the creeds of the Christian faith up to this day. He also wrote the Athanasian Creed.

- Through the ploy of Arius and his followers, Athanasius was exiled five times, but in the end, he prevailed and set Christianity on the right footing.

Origen of Alexandria (c.185–c.254), an Egyptian

Origen of Alexandria was an Egyptian and one of the early Christian scholars. He was a theologian, and it is said that he gave lectures in Rome, Caesarea, and Jerusalem and that he corrected the Septuagint because he knew Hebrew. Clement of Alexandria was his teacher.

Clement of Alexandria (Date of birth unknown. Died about 215 AD)

Titus Flavius Clemens is called Clement of Alexandria to distinguish him from Clement of Rome. He was the head of the catechetical school of Alexandria and a Greek theologian. He composed the "Hortatory Discourse to the Greeks" (*Protreptikos pros Ellenas*), a persuasive appeal for the faith in which, among other things, he maintained that "Man is born for God. The Word calls men to Himself. The full truth is found in Christ alone [and] (t)he work ends with a description of the God-fearing Christian. He answers those who urge that it is wrong to desert one's ancestral religion.[8]

Cyril of Alexandria (c.378–444 AD)

Cyril was the bishop of Alexandria. He was born in Alexandria, Egypt, and was African and black. He was chosen to be head of the Egyptian church after his uncle Theophilus died in 412 AD. During the theological dispute that caused a break between Alexandria and Constantinople, Cyril brilliantly defended the orthodox belief that Christ is "a single eternally divine person who also became incarnate as man."[9] According to a monk named Nestorius, the title of "Mother of God" ("Theotokos") ascribed to Mary, mother of Jesus, was wrong. He insisted that Mary should be given the title "Christotokos," meaning "Mother of Christ," because he thought Mary could not have given birth to God. If his position were accepted, which the theologians of the church in Antioch did, then Christ would not have been fully God and fully man since his doctrine basically denied the God-ness of Christ. Cyril of Alexandria successfully defended the Alexandrian position at the Council of Ephesus (June 22–July 31, 431) resulting in Nestorius being condemned and deposed as patriarch and later suffering exile. Cyril was declared Doctor of the Church in 1883. He has been declared a saint by the Roman Catholic Church and is celebrated by the Roman Catholic Church on June 27 and the Eastern churches on June 9.

Other Blacks in the Annals of Church History

Tertullian (c.160–220 AD)

Tertullian, an African born in Carthage, Tunisia, in North Africa, was an early prolific Christian author. He was a "Christian theologian, polemicist, [and] moralist who, as the initiator of ecclesiastical Latin, was instrumental in shaping the vocabulary and thought of Western Christianity."[40] The following quotes are attributed to Tertullian, also known as Quintus Septimius Florens Tertullianus:

+ The blood of the martyrs is the seed of the church.

+ It is certain because it is impossible.

+ Hope is patience with the lamp lit.

+ The first reaction to truth is hatred.

+ Divorce these days is a religious vow, as if the proper offspring of marriage.

+ Nothing that is God's is obtainable by money.

+ Indeed heresies are themselves instigated by philosophy.

+ See how these Christians love one another.

+ What has Athens to do with Jerusalem?

+ You can judge the quality of their faith from the way they behave. Discipline is an index to doctrine.

Tertullian was a lawyer.

Simon, who carried the cross for Jesus

Simon showed up when Jesus could no longer carry the cross to Golgotha. He was passing by from the country at the very time that Jesus could no longer carry the cross, and the soldiers forcing him to carry it for Him was God-ordained (Luke 23:26ff). God actually sent Simon of Cyrene to help Jesus carry the cross. (Cyrene was an ancient Greek city in Libya in North Africa). Simeon the Niger mentioned in Acts 13:1 and Simon of Cyrene who carried the cross for Jesus are one and the same person. Simeon is a push name for Simon, and it was probably given to Simon of Cyrene in Antioch out of admiration for carrying the cross for Jesus and his subsequent work in the church.

Obviously Simon of Cyrene became a believer when the church was established, joined it, and went to Antioch where the first

Gentile church was planted and where the followers of Jesus were first called Christians (Acts 11:19–26). His firsthand experience of Jesus's suffering bear witness. Acts 11:19–20 says, "Now those who were scattered after the persecution that arose over Stephen traveled as far as Phoenicia, Cyprus, and Antioch, preaching the word to no one but the Jews only. But some of them were men from Cyprus and *Cyrene*, who, when they had come to Antioch, spoke to the Hellenists, preaching the Lord Jesus" (emphasis mine).

In Antioch, he became a teacher or a prophet and was called Simeon the Niger because he was black. The word "Niger" is a Latin adjective meaning black and had no derogative connotations at that time. So he was called Simeon the Black. A black man therefore carried the cross for Jesus, who was crucified by the Romans goaded by the Jews, when in His purely human form, He could no longer carry it. That black man became a teacher or prophet in the early church.

Alexander and Rufus

Alexander and Rufus mentioned in Mark 15:21 were also black men. They were sons of Simon of Cyrene and prominent among the Roman Christians. Rufus is mentioned also in Romans 16:13 where it is said he was "chosen in the Lord."

The Ethiopian Eunuch

The Ethiopian Eunuch is not identified by name. But the Holy Bible says he was an official in the service of Candace, queen of Ethiopia. Shortly after Jesus's death and resurrection, the eunuch came from Ethiopia to Jerusalem to worship the God of Israel. He was converted to Christianity on his way back to Ethiopia. Following is the biblical narrative of his conversion:

Acts 8:26–39 (ESV)

Now an angel of the Lord said to Philip, "Rise and go toward the south to the road that goes down from Jerusalem to Gaza." This is a desert place. And he rose and went. And there was an

Ethiopian, a eunuch, a court official of Candace, queen of the Ethiopians, who was in charge of all her treasure. He had come to Jerusalem to worship and was returning, seated in his chariot, and he was reading the prophet Isaiah. And the Spirit said to Philip, "Go over and join this chariot." So Philip ran to him and heard him reading Isaiah the prophet and asked, "Do you understand what you are reading?" And he said," How can I, unless someone guides me?" And he invited Philip to come up and sit with him. Now the passage of the Scripture that he was reading was this:

> "Like a sheep he was led to the slaughter and like a lamb before its shearer is silent, so he opens not his mouth. In his humiliation justice was denied him. Who can describe his generation?

> For his life is taken away from the earth."

And the eunuch said to Philip, "About whom, I ask you, does the prophet say this, about himself or about someone else?" Then Philip opened his mouth, and beginning with this Scripture he told him the good news about Jesus. And as they were going along the road they came to some water, and the eunuch said, "See, here is water! What prevents me from being baptized?" And he commanded the chariot to stop, and they both went down into the water, Philip and the eunuch, and he baptized him. And when they came up out of the water, the Spirit of the Lord carried Philip away, and the eunuch saw him no more, and went on his way rejoicing.

So the good news through and salvation by the seed of the woman got back to Africa through a black man almost immediately after it exploded.

William Joseph Seymour (May 2, 1870–September 28, 1922)

In 1906, a one-eyed black man called William Joseph Seymour caused what has become known as the Azusa Street Revival in which great miracles were performed. It was through that revival that we now have the Assemblies of God church, the Baptist Church, the Holiness Pentecostals, and other evangelical churches. The Presbyterian and Methodist churches were also revived as a result of that revival.

During the time of William Seymour, the United States of America was under segregation in which blacks were not allowed to attend the same schools and could not even live in the same communities with whites. There were laws popularly known as Jim Crow laws segregating the people. It is said that William Seymour could not attend Sunday school with the Christian whites so he would sit in the corridor and listen to the teachings. He grew a hunger for God, and so with fervent prayer, sometimes with other people, God visited America through this one-eyed black man. And this black man ordained ministers, including whites. The Pentecostal movement he started by the power of the Holy Spirit has spread throughout the world with "an estimated 279 million classical Pentecostals, making 4 percent of the total world population and 12.8 percent of the world's Christian population Pentecostal."[24]

Dr. Martin Luther King

Dr. Martin Luther King, born Michael Luther King Jr. and also known as Martin Luther King Jr., was a Baptist preacher who was instrumental in freeing American blacks who were under the yoke of oppression as a result of slavery and Jim Crow laws. He was a co-pastor of Ebenezer Baptist Church in Atlanta, Georgia, serving with his father. He also served as the pastor of Dexter Avenue Baptist Church in Montgomery, Alabama, and was an outstanding civil rights leader. "In the eleven- year period between 1957 and 1968, King traveled over six million miles and spoke over twenty-five hundred times, appearing wherever there was injustice, protest, and action; and meanwhile he wrote five books as well as numerous articles."[21] While at the Crozer Theological Seminary in Pennsylvania, he was elected president of a predominantly white senior class. He is fondly remembered for his "I Have a Dream" speech in Washington, DC, at which about 250,000 people attended. He was assassinated in 1968 due to his work in the liberation of the oppressed blacks."[22]

CHAPTER 9

MARY, THE MOTHER OF GOD

ary, the woman through whom Jesus Christ of Nazareth came into the world, was black, or dark- skinned. Have you ever heard of the Black Madonna? It is the painting or statue of the Virgin Mary and infant Jesus depicted with black skin. The original painting of Mary is said to have been done by St. Luke, who wrote the gospel of Luke and the book of Acts. It is universally agreed that St. Luke actually interviewed Mary before writing his gospel. That is why he says in Luke 1:3–4, "it seemed good to me also, having had perfect understanding of all things from the very first, to write to you an orderly account, most excellent Theophilus, that you may know the certainty of those things in which you were instructed." It is believed that he was drawing Mary on a table made by the Lord and Savior Jesus Christ while interviewing her and he drew her black! Also, almost all the early statues of Virgin Mary are made with black wood. Monique Scheer states,

> other Italian images attributed to St. Luke appear to have been known as dark at least in some circles in the sixteenth century or even earlier. In 1571, the Dominican Gabriel de Barletta cites not only a thirteenth-century authority on the question of the Virgin's complexion but also images renowned as true portraits, which he describes as dark: You ask: Was the Virgin dark or fair? Albertus Magnus says that she was not simply dark, nor simply red-haired, nor just fair-haired … Mary was a blend of complexions, partaking of all of them, because a face partaking of all of them is a beautiful one … And yet this, says Albertus, we must admit: she was

a little on the dark side. There are three reasons for thinking this-firstly by reason of complexion, since Jews tend to be dark and she was a Jewess; secondly by reason of witness, since St. Luke made the three pictures of her now at Rome, Loreto and Bologna, and these are brown-complexioned; thirdly, by reason of affinity. A son commonly takes after his mother, and vice versa; Christ was dark, therefore … [36] Leonard Moss cites the Scots Catechism of 1552 as a direct reference to black madonnas: "[these statues] darkened into something not far from idolatry … when … one image of the Virgin [generally a black or ugly one] was regarded as more powerful for the help of suppliants."[37] A Mirakelbuch from Altotting of 1674, about the same time as Gumppenberg's work, mentions nothing of the madonna's blackness in the text, but the copperplate rontispiece is highly suggestive of a dark complexion.[29]

If the Virgin Mary had dark skin and her conception was of the Holy Spirit who has no skin color, then what was the earthly skin color of her Son, Jesus Christ? He had to be black, or dark-skinned, right? No wonder He came to His own but His own rejected Him (John 1:11). In fact, a painting of Jesus Christ in the Coptic Church in Egypt depicts Jesus and His disciples with black skin. The Coptic Church in Egypt is said to have been planted in 42 AD by St. Mark who wrote the gospel of Mark just about nine or ten years after Jesus's death and resurrection during the time that Rome ruled Egypt in fulfillment of Isaiah's prophecy in Isaiah 19:19–22,

> In that day there will be an altar to the LORD in the midst of the land of Egypt, and a pillar to the LORD at its border. And it will be for a sign and for a witness to the LORD of hosts in the land of Egypt; for they will cry to the LORD because of the oppressors, and He will send them a Savior and a Mighty One, and He will deliver them. Then the LORD will be known to Egypt, and the Egyptians will know the LORD in that day, and will make sacrifice and offering; yes, they will make a vow to the LORD and perform *it*. And the LORD will strike Egypt, He will strike and heal *it;* they will return to the LORD,

and He will be entreated by them and heal them. (italics in the original)

Mary appeared several times in Scripture in various forms before finally appearing as Mary the Virgin just as her seed appeared several times in Scripture before finally appearing as Jesus, the Christ. Among others, Mary appeared as Rehab the Inn Keeper (harlot) who saved the Hebrew spies who surveyed the fortified city of Jericho, making it possible for the Hebrews to take the city (Joshua 2), and who eventually married Boaz. She was planted among the Canaanites of Jericho on top of the city wall by God Himself to protect the Hebrew spies and give that two-person Recce Regiment valuable information so the Hebrews could conquer that fortified city just as Moses was planted in the house of Pharaoh to learn the arts and wisdom of the Egyptians so he could eventually conquer them. Mary also appeared as Ruth the Moabite who forsook her people and clung to Naomi and ultimately married Obed (book of Ruth). Both Rehab and Ruth became ancestors of Jesus Christ.

Jesus also, among others, appeared as the Rock that followed the children of Israel during the exodus (the church in the wilderness), which God instructed Moses to strike with his staff for water to come out for the Israelites to drink, which he did. On a second occasion to speak to it for water to come out, he struck it again (twice) in anger. On both occasions, water gushed out for the children of Israel to drink (Exodus 17:1–7; Numbers 20:8–11; 1 Corinthians 10:3–4), but Moses' disobedience on the second occasion cost him his entry into the Promised Land. He also appeared as a man to Joshua during the siege of Jericho (Joshua 5:13–15). We know it was Jesus who appeared to Joshua because when Joshua stood before Him and asked, "*Are* You for us or for our adversaries?" (italics in the original), He answered, "No, but *as* Commander of the army of the LORD I have now come" (emphasis in the original). And when Joshua fell on his face and worshipped, He accepted the worship. Angels do not accept worship (Revelation 19:10). And again when Joshua asked Him "What does my Lord say to His servant?" He replied "Take your sandal off your foot, for the place where you stand *is* holy" (emphasis in the original). (See Exodus 3:5.) And Joshua did so.

CHAPTER 10

RIVERS IN AFRICA IN THE BOOK OF GENESIS

The Land of the Blacks (Africa)

Genesis 2:7–14 (Amplified Bible) reads,

> *Then the Lord God formed man from the dust of the ground and breathed into his nostrils the breath or spirit of life, and man became a living being. And the Lord God planted a garden toward the east, in Eden [delight]; and there He put the man whom He had formed (framed, constituted). And out of the ground the Lord God made to grow every tree that is pleasant to the sight or to be desired—good (suitable, pleasant) for food; the tree of life also in the center of the garden, and the tree of the knowledge of [the difference between] good and evil and blessing and calamity.* **Now a river went out of Eden to water the garden; and from there it divided and became four [river] heads.** *The first is named Pishon; it is the one flowing around the whole land of Havilah, where there is gold. The gold of that land is of high quality; bdellium (pearl?) and onyx stone are there.* **The second river is named Gihon; it is the one flowing around the whole land of Cush.** *The third river is named Hiddekel [the Tigris]; it is the one flowing east of Assyria. And the fourth river is the Euphrates. (emphasis added)*

Genesis 2:13 (KJV) states, *"And the name of the second river is Gihon: the same is it that compasseth the whole land of Ethiopia"* (emphasis added).

As seen earlier, from creation through the flood of Noah up to the days the earth was divided, the four riverheads that parted from the river that went out of the garden of Eden flowed through Havilah, which comprised the western part of present-day Africa and the entire present-day South America and a small part of North America and through the land of Cush, which comprised a greater part of present-day Africa, part of the Middle East, and part of Europe and Asia (see figure 2). The land of Havilah and the land of Cush were not referred to as Africa or South America; nor were they referred to as Middle East, Europe, or Asia before the earth was divided. As already noted, they were referred to as Egypt, the land Havilah, the land of Cush, Ethiopia, and the land of Ham (Genesis 2:11, 13; Psalm 78:51, 105:23–27, 106:21–22). That is the reason why the name "Africa" is not found in the Bible.

Rivers in the Land of Havilah and the Land of Cush

Havilah was the name of the original person whose name part of the land in southern Africa, part of West Africa, the entire land of South America, and a small part of North America bore at the beginning of creation and whose namesake Cush's son bore. Cush was also the name of the original person whose namesake, the son of Ham, bore after the flood and before the earth was divided (see figures 1 and 3).

After the earth was divided, the topography of the earth changed. Mountains formed where there were none, and valleys were created where none existed before. The catchment area of the Pishon, Gihon, Hiddekel, and Euphrates, which was in the garden of Eden, was cut off when the garden of Eden was probably buried in the Black Sea. Since the source of the four riverheads was cut off and because the topography of the earth had changed, the Pishon took its source from the highlands of northeastern Zambia between Lakes Tanganyika and Malawi and flows into the Atlantic Ocean and became known as the Congo River. Likewise, the part of the Pishon River, which was in present-day South America, became the Amazon River that runs through Peru, Ecuador, Venezuela, Colombia, Brazil, and Bolivia before emptying into the Atlantic Ocean. Its source has not been agreed upon by scholars, whereas some say its source is the

Apurimac River in Peru; others say the source is Mount Huagra and so on.[16] The dried riverbed of the Pishon beginning from the river that went out of the Garden of Eden before it was cut off has not been discovered yet, or maybe it has been completely obliterated for reasons best known to the Creator. The Gihon became the Nile River, took its source from the Ethiopian highlands, and flowed north into the Mediterranean Sea due to the same reasons given above. The Hiddekel (Tigris) and Euphrates also took their sources from eastern Turkey and empty into the Persian Gulf. Of the four riverheads, only the Euphrates has maintained its ancient name up to this day, maybe to make it easy for posterity to know the truth of the biblical narratives (see figure 5).

Here is what Encyclopedia Britannica has to say about the Congo River:

> **Congo River,** formerly **Zaire River,** river in west-central Africa. With a length of 2,900 miles (4,700 km), it is the continent's second longest river, after the Nile. It rises in the highlands of northeastern Zambia between Lakes Tanganyika and Nyasa (Malawi) as the Chambeshi River at an elevation of 5,760 feet (1,760 metres) above sea level and at a distance of about 430 miles (700 km) from the Indian Ocean. Its course then takes the form of a giant counterclockwise arc, flowing to the northwest, west, and southwest before draining into the Atlantic Ocean at Banana (Banane) in the Democratic Republic of the Congo. Its drainage basin, covering an area of 1,335,000 square miles (3,457,000 square km), takes in almost the entire territory of that country, as well as most of the Republic of the Congo, the Central African Republic, eastern Zambia, and northern Angola and parts of Cameroon and Tanzania.[27]

The Nile is also known as the Blue Nile and White Nile in some countries. It flows through twelve countries in Africa, namely Egypt, Sudan, South Sudan, Eritrea, Ethiopia, Central African Republic, Kenya, Uganda, Rwanda, Burundi, Congo, and Tanzania. Here is what Encyclopedia Britannica says about the Blue Nile in Ethiopia:

> **Blue Nile River**, Arabic **Al-Nīl Al-Azraq** or **Al-Baḥr Al-Azraq,** Amharic **Abāy**, headstream of the Nile River and source of almost 70 percent of its floodwater at Khartoum. It reputedly rises as the Abāy from a spring 6,000 feet (1,800 metres) above sea level, near Lake Tana in northwestern Ethiopia … By far the greater part of the Blue Nile's waters come from such tributaries as the Dinder and Rahad rivers, which rise in the Ethiopian highlands.[12]

Of the Nile River in Egypt here is what Encyclopedia Britannica says:

> **Nile River,** Arabic **Baḥr Al-Nīl** or **Nahr Al-Nīl**, river, the father of African rivers and the longest river in the world. It rises south of the Equator and flows northward through northeastern Africa to drain into the Mediterranean Sea. It has a length of about 4,132 miles (6,650 kilometres) and drains an area estimated at 1,293,000 square miles (3,349,000 square kilometres). Its basin includes parts of Tanzania, Burundi, Rwanda, the Democratic Republic of the Congo, Kenya, Uganda, South Sudan, Ethiopia, Sudan, and the cultivated part of Egypt. Its most distant source is the Kagera River in Burundi.

The Nile is formed by three principal streams: the Blue Nile (Arabic: Al-Baḥr Al-Azraq; Amhari c: Abay) and the Atbara (Arabic: Nahr ʿAṭbarah), which flow from the highlands of Ethiopia, and the White Nile (Arabic: Al-Baḥr Al-Abyad), the headstreams of which flow into Lakes Victoria and Albert. The name Nile is derived from the Greek Neilos (Latin: Nilus), which probably originated from the Semitic root *nahal*, meaning a valley or a river valley and hence, by an extension of the meaning, a river."[15] The previous entries emphasize the assertion that the Pishon River and Gihon River in Genesis 2:12–13 are the same as the Congo River and Nile River (Blue and White) and both of them are in Africa to this day. Egypt is and has always been part of Africa, not the Middle East, as some people are asserting now.

Conclusion

It is written in 1 Corinthians 1:27–29 that God chooses the foolish things of the world to confound the wise. He chooses the weak things of the world to confound those things that are mighty. The base things of the world, things that are despised, and things that are not, He has chosen to bring about the things that are so no flesh should glory in His presence. He is not a man that He should lie (Numbers 23:19), and His foolishness is wiser than the wisdom of men (1 Corinthians 1:25). His ways are mysterious. His ways are not like mankind's ways, and He is not a respecter of persons. He works with whom He will work and casts aside whom He will cast aside. No one can determine His ways of doing things. The best His people can do is to find out what He is doing and do it with Him. But most of the time those He created in His own image and likeness disobey Him. But He knows they are dust so He does not reward them according to their iniquities (Psalm 103:9–10). He knew from the beginning what would become of man so He made provision for his redemption before He created him.

Through mysterious ways, sometimes sounding ridiculous, He finally brought His salvation plan to fruition. Through former idol worshippers like Abram, disobedient egoistic individuals like Pharaoh, innkeepers (or harlots) like Rehab, pleasantly stubborn widows like Ruth the Moabite, a rock, blacks, and others, God has brought His church to where it is today. Blacks' contribution to church history has been tremendous. It is not possible to list all the blacks who contributed their quota to church history in this little book. But we have counted and are still counting. Are you involved?

APPENDIXES

The Apostles' Creed

I believe in God, the Father almighty,

creator of heaven and earth.

I believe in Jesus Christ, his only Son, our Lord,

who was conceived by the Holy Spirit

and born of the virgin Mary.

He suffered under Pontius Pilate,

was crucified, died, and was buried;

he descended to hell.

The third day he rose again from the dead.

He ascended to heaven

and is seated at the right hand of God the Father almighty.

From there he will come to judge the living and the dead.

I believe in the Holy Spirit,

the holy catholic[3] church,

the communion of saints,

the forgiveness of sins,

the resurrection of the body,

and the life everlasting. Amen.

---

[3] Catholic, wherever it appears, means universal, not the Roman Catholic Church. Catholic means universal. The Roman Catholic Church is a unit of the universal church, just as any other church is.

The Athanasian Creed

Whoever desires to be saved should above all hold to the catholic faith.

Anyone who does not keep it whole and unbroken will doubtless perish eternally.

Now this is the catholic faith:

That we worship one God in trinity and the trinity in unity,

neither blending their persons

nor dividing their essence.

For the person of the Father is a distinct person,

the person of the Son is another,

and that of the Holy Spirit still another.

But the divinity of the Father, Son, and Holy Spirit is one,

their glory equal, their majesty coeternal.

What quality the Father has, the Son has, and the Holy Spirit has.

The Father is uncreated,

the Son is uncreated,

the Holy Spirit is uncreated.

The Father is immeasurable,

the Son is immeasurable,

the Holy Spirit is immeasurable.

The Father is eternal,

the Son is eternal,

the Holy Spirit is eternal.

And yet there are not three eternal beings;

there is but one eternal being.

So too there are not three uncreated or immeasurable beings;

there is but one uncreated and immeasurable being.

Similarly, the Father is almighty, the Son is almighty,

the Holy Spirit is almighty.

Yet there are not three almighty beings;

there is but one almighty being.

Thus the Father is God,

the Son is God,

the Holy Spirit is God.

Yet there are not three gods;

there is but one God.

Thus the Father is Lord,

the Son is Lord,

the Holy Spirit is Lord.

Yet there are not three lords;

there is but one Lord.

Just as Christian truth compels us

to confess each person individually

as both God and Lord,

so catholic religion forbids us

to say that there are three gods or lords.

The Father was neither made nor created nor begotten from anyone.

The Son was neither made nor created;

he was begotten from the Father alone.

The Holy Spirit was neither made nor created nor begotten;

he proceeds from the Father and the Son.

Accordingly there is one Father, not three fathers;

there is one Son, not three sons;

there is one Holy Spirit, not three holy spirits.

Nothing in this trinity is before or after,

nothing is greater or smaller;

in their entirety the three persons

are coeternal and coequal with each other.

So in everything, as was said earlier,

we must worship their trinity in their unity

and their unity in their trinity.

Anyone then who desires to be saved

should think thus about the trinity.

But it is necessary for eternal salvation

that one also believe in the incarnation

of our Lord Jesus Christ faithfully.

Now this is the true faith:

That we believe and confess

that our Lord Jesus Christ, God's Son,

is both God and human, equally.

He is God from the essence of the Father,

begotten before time;

and he is human from the essence of his mother,

born in time;

completely God, completely human,

with a rational soul and human flesh;

equal to the Father as regards divinity,

less than the Father as regards humanity.

Although he is God and human,

yet Christ is not two, but one.

He is one, however,

not by his divinity being turned into flesh,

but by God's taking humanity to himself.

He is one,

certainly not by the blending of his essence,

but by the unity of his person.

For just as one human is both rational soul and flesh,

so too the one Christ is both God and human.

He suffered for our salvation;

he descended to hell;

he arose from the dead;

he ascended to heaven;

he is seated at the Father's right hand;

from there he will come to judge the living and the dead.

At his coming all people will arise bodily

and give an accounting of their own deeds.

Those who have done good will enter eternal life,

and those who have done evil will enter eternal fire.

This is the catholic faith: one cannot be saved without believing it firmly and faithfully.

The Nicene Creed

We believe in one God,

the Father almighty,

maker of heaven and earth,

of all things visible and invisible.

And in one Lord Jesus Christ,

the only Son of God,

begotten from the Father before all ages,

God from God,

Light from Light,

true God from true God,

begotten, not made;

of the same essence as the Father.

Through him all things were made.

For us and for our salvation

he came down from heaven;

he became incarnate by the Holy Spirit and the virgin Mary,

and was made human.

He was crucified for us under Pontius Pilate;

he suffered and was buried.

The third day he rose again, according to the Scriptures.

He ascended to heaven

and is seated at the right hand of the Father.

He will come again with glory

to judge the living and the dead.

His kingdom will never end.

And we believe in the Holy Spirit,

the Lord, the giver of life.

He proceeds from the Father and the Son,

and with the Father and the Son is worshiped and glorified.

He spoke through the prophets.

We believe in one holy catholic and apostolic church.

We affirm one baptism for the forgiveness of sins.

We look forward to the resurrection of the dead,

and to life in the world to come. Amen.

Bibliography

1). Bet Yeshurun Messianic Assembly. *Was Sarah the Sister and Wife of Abraham?* 2020. http://www.messianics.us/bible-history/sarah-and-abraham.html. 29 November 2020.

2). "Ethiopia," Easton's Bible Dictionary. https://www.biblestudytools.com/dictionary/ethiopia/. 2 9 2021.

3). Bible Gateway. *Amplified Bible (AMP).* n.d. https://www.biblegateway.com/passage/?search=Genesis+2%3A7-14&version=AMP. 29 May 2020.

4). Bible Gateway. *Genesis 6, King James Version.* n.d. https://www.biblegateway.com/passage/?search=Genesis%206&version=KJV. 28 May 2020.

5). —. *Revelation 13:8.* n.d. https://www.biblegateway.com/passage/?search=Revelation+13%3A8&version=NLT;MSG;ESV;NIV. 29 May 2020.

6). Biblebelievers.org.au. *PART TWO: THE LENEAGE OF HAM.* n.d. http://www.biblebelievers.org.au/nation02.htm#Table%202.%20THE%20LINEAGE%20 OF%20HAM. 9 9 2021. <https://www.biblebelievers.org.au>.

7). BibleGateway. *Genesis 9.* 2011. https://www.biblegateway.com/passage/?search=Genesis%209&version=NIV. 2 9 2021.

8). Catholic Encyclopedia. *Clemant of Alexandria.* n.d. https://www.catholic.com/encyclopedia/clement-of-alexandria. 19 1 2019.

9). Catholic News Agency. *St. Cyril of Alexandria.* n.d. https://www. catholicnewsagency.com/saint/st-cyril-of-alexandria-516. 19 1 2019.

10). Christianity Today. *Athanasius / Christian History.* 2 August 2008.   https://www.christianitytoday.com/history/people/ theologians/athanasius.html. 8 January 2019. <https://www. christianitytoday.com>.

11). —. *Christian History, Athanasius.* 8 August 2008. https://www. christianitytoday.com/history/people/theologians/athanasius. html. 8 January 2019.

12). Encyclopedia Britannica. *The Blue Nile.* 5 3 2014. <http://www. britannica.com/EBchecked/topic/70320/Blue-Nile-River>.

13). Hapgood, Charles H. *Maps of the Ancient Sea Kings: Evidence of Advanced Civilization in the Ice Age, 1966, Revised Edition.* New York: E. P. Dutton, 1979.

14). Harvey, Ian. *Wingate News.* 2 January 2018. https://www. thevintagenews.com/2018/01/02/piri-reis-map-of-1513/. 5 June 2020. <https://www.thevintagenews.com/2018/01/02/piri-reis- map-of-1513/>.

15). Hurst, Harold Edwin. *River Nile.* 16 4 2014. <http://www. britannica.com/EBchecked/topic/415347/Nile-River>.

16). Kiprop, Joseph. *What Is The Source Of The River Amazon?* 10 May 2018. https://www.worldatlas.com/articles/what-is-the- source-of-the-river-amazon.html. 5 12 2020.

17). Mallowan, Max. *Nineveh, ANCIENT CITY, IRAQ.* 6 September 2018. https://www.britannica.com/place/Nineveh-ancient-city- Iraq. 4 9 2021. <https://www.britannica.com/place/Nineveh- ancient-city-Iraq>.

18). Muhammad, Wesley, PhD. *Black Arabia & The African Origin of Islam, 2009, 2nd ed.,.* Atlanta: A-Team Publishing, 2009 Print (book).

19). National Geographic. *Ozone layer*. 9 May 2011. https://www.nationalgeographic.org/encyclopedia/ozone-layer/. 7 9 2021.

20). National Geographic Society. *Family Reference Atlas of the World*. Washingtton, D. C.: National Geographic Partners, 2010, 16-17. Print (book)

21). NobelPrize.org.Nobel Prize Outreach AB. *Martin Luther King Jr., Biographical*. 7 February 2020. <https://www.nobelprize.org/prizes/peace/1964/king/biographical/>. 7 February 2020. <<https://www.nobelprize.org/prizes/peace/1964/king/biographical/>>.

22). —. *Martin Luther King, Jr. - Biography*. 13 September 2021. <https://www.nobelprize.org/prizes/peace/1964/king/biographical/>. 13 September 2021. <https://www.nobelprize.org/prizes/peace/1964/king/biographical/>.

23). Patterson, Tom. *World Political Map*. n.d. http://www.shadedrelief.com/political/Political_Map_NE.jpg. 27 3 2021.

24). Pentecostalism - Statistics and Denominations. *Statistics and Denominations*. 2020. https://www.liquisearch.com/pentecostalism/statistics_and_denominations. 3 12 2020.

25). Pietrobon, Massimo. *Map of Pangaea with Modern-Day Borders*. n.d.

26). —. *PANGEA POLITICA* . 4 August 2012. http://capitan-mas-ideas.blogspot.com/2012/08/pangea-politica.html. 7 6 2020.

27). Pourtier, R. and G. F. Sautter. *Congo River*. n.d. https://www.britannica.com/place/Congo-River/Physical-features. 3 12 2020. <http://www.britannica.com/EBchecked/topic/132484/Congo-River>.

28). Sauter, Magan. *Bible History Daily*. 13 10 2018. <https//www.biblicalarchaecology.org>. 05 1 2019. <https://www.bblicalarchaeology.org>.

29). Scheer, Monique. "From Majesty to Mystery: Change in the Meanings of Black Madonna from the Sixteenth to Nineteenth Centuries." Scheer, Monique. *From Majesty to Mystery: Change in the Meanings of Black Madonna from the Sixteenth to Nineteenth Centuries*. The American Historica Review, 107 (5), 2002. 1412-1440. http://www.academicroom.com/article/ majesty-mystery-change-meanings-black- madonnas-sixteenth- nineteenth-centuries.

30). Sheknows Media, LLC. *Baby Names/Abel*. n.d. https://www. sheknows.com/baby- names/name/abel/. 4 9 2021.

31). St...Steemit.com, Pangea and the days of Peleg -. *Pangea and the days of Peleg - St...Steemit.com*. 2019. Monday November 2019. <https://steemit.com/opinion/@towjam/pangea-and-the-days-of-peleg>.

32). Strong, James. *The New Strong's Exhautive Concordance of the Bible, Comfort Print Edition*. Nashville: Thomas Nelson Publishers, 1995. Print.

33). SUNNUBIAN. *10 Arguments That Prove Ancient Egyptians Were Black*. 10 November 2013. <https://www.africanamerican. org/topic/10-arguments-that-prove-ancient-   egyptians-were-black>. 27 December 2019. <https://www.africanamerica.org/ topic/10- arguments-that-prove-ancient-egyptians-were-black>.

34). The Editors of Encyclopaedia Britannica. *Balthasar, Legendary Figure*. 2021. https://www.britannica.com/topic/Balthasar. 9 September 2021. <https://msu.edu>.

35). —. *Eusebius of Nicomedia BISHOP*. Vers. https://www. britannica,com. 20 July 1998. https://www.britannica.com/ biography/Eusebius-of-Nicomedia. 06 1 2019.

36). Thomas Nelson, Inc. *The Holy Bible, New King James Version*. China: Thomas Nelson, Inc., 2013.

37). —. *The Holy Bible, New King James Verson*. Nashville: Thomas Nelson, Inc., 2013. Print (book)

38). —. *The Holy Bible, New King James Verson.* Nasville: Thomas Nelson, Inc., 2013. Print (book printed in China).

39). wikiwikiyarou. *Reconstruction of the Ziggurat of Ur Uploaded by Jan van der Crabben.* 26 April 2012. https://www.ancient.eu/image/198/reconstruction-of-the-ziggurat-of-ur/. 27 3 2021.

40). Wilken, Robert L. *Tertullian CHRSTIAN THEOLOGIAN.* n.d. https://www.britannica.com/biography/Tertullian. 17 1 2019. <https:..www.britanica.com>.

BIOGRAPHY

Emmanuel Kofi Bonney, formerly known as Franklin Kofi Bonney, is a Pastor, a Chartered Accountant (Ghana), and an International Accountant (UK). He holds a Master of Ministry degree from the Graduate School of Southwestern Christian University, (Oklahoma City, OK, USA); a Bachelor of Arts degree (*summa cum laude*) in biblical education from Beulah Heights University, (Atlanta, GA, USA); and a Master of Science degree in accounting obtained from the Graduate School of Kaplan University (Chicago, IL, USA). A devout Christian who has been working in the Lord's vineyard since 1979, he is currently trying to plant a church that will hold nonstop services around the clock. He lives with his wife, Edith.